Indelible Ink

Helen Iles

 A catalogue record for this
book is available from the
National Library of Australia

Copyright © 2017 Helen Iles
All rights reserved.
ISBN: 1876922869
ISBN-13: 9781876922863

Published by Linellen Press
265 Boomerang Road
Oldbury, Western Australia
Website: www.linellenpress.com

Dedication

Dedicated to my husband and best friend, Lindsay.
Thank you for supporting my need to write.

Contents

Dedication iii

Contents v

Acknowledgments vii

All in the Family 1

Any Place 4

A Time For Dawn 7

Battle Beach – 6th of June. 16

Behind the Scenes 18

Brave Molly 24

Crocs on the Highway 27

Devachan 35

From a Blanket 36

From the Steps of Bradley Street 37

hoops 42

In Bradley's House 44

Island Time 51

Just a Doll and a Story 58

Kimberley Dream 64

Listen 66

Moments 67

Much Ado About Nunning 73

Neither Lie, Douglas 86

On 66th Street 89

Resolutions 101

Riding On Trains 104

Serpent River 107

Study Time 109

The Birthday 112

The Breaker's Walk 117

The Cattle Dog 119

The Eagle 126

The Horse from Ethel Creek 128

The Power of the Sea 134

The Prince of Wails 135
The Magic of Christmas 139
The Remember Game 141
The Trouvere and the Troubadour 147
Wild Roses 149
Achievements 153
About the Author 156

Acknowledgments

I would like to acknowledge the many different writing organisations across Australia that hold competitions to encourage writers to produce quality writing. These opportunities are the reason these collective pieces were written and subsequently awarded by either prize, publication or both.

All in the Family

The halls of Gollen Manor were dark even though the moon was high and full in the sky outside. Maybe it was the tall, narrow windows looking out from the Gothic facade that prevented the light intruding; maybe it was the clouds. More likely though it was the moon's own reluctance to enter the house, for nothing pleasant was happening in the manor-house that night; certainly nothing the moon would want to reveal.

Shielded by the cupboard in the darkened hallway, Eva stood trembling, the sheerness of her nightgown doing little to ease the chill on her skin as a cold wind blew across her. But there was more than just the cold night air and the still darkness of midnight to chill her: Paul was searching the house. She could hear his footsteps, muffled as they were, on the strip of carpet that protected the floor round the hearth.

Listening a while longer, she realised he had moved further across the room, his footsteps sounding more distant as he skirted the Victorian bureau which had belonged to her grandfather.

She shuddered again, her flesh crawling at the reason Paul sought her.

"Eva? Where are you?" His voice drifted down the long hallway, soft with caution; soft with encouragement. "Come out, Eva. I'm here to help you."

Help me, be damned, she thought. If Paul finds me I'll be as dead as the other poor unfortunates -- all of whom had been murdered in their beds. Her eyes narrowed momentarily as she recalled the blood dripping to a pool on the carpet, the steady drip coming from cousin Maisie's hand. She knew that it would stop soon for Maisie was dead, her throat opened to a gaping slit, her hand having obviously gone to contain the flow in her shock.

"Eva?"

Forcing back the vision, she glanced with caution down the passage. Paul was getting nearer. She looked around. There were two doors close to her – one on the wall by which she was standing, the other allowing access to a room beneath the high wooden stairway. She wondered if she could reach one of them before Paul saw her, before he eliminated all other hiding places in his bid to find her.

She made to move, but it was too late. Paul was entering the passage further down. If she moved now he would see her for sure, so she stayed where she was and waited, her pulse racing, her heart pounding hard beats beneath her chest, the thuds so loud she was sure Paul would hear her.

"Eva? I know you're down there."

Shivering again, her eyes widened in the darkness. But how could he know that? she worried. How could he be so sure she was there? She had made it to this place while he was still upstairs, while he was so busy going from room to room. She took a second to imagine his handiwork; how he would have opened each door in turn, unaware of what awaited him on the other side. And she knew he would not leave until a sheet was covering the corpse he left behind.

He was in Uncle Albert's room when she had managed to slip by him without a sound, the stairway allowing silent passage to the floor below. How she had sighed with relief at that. How close she had come to being caught. It would only take Paul to turn around and see her and all would have been lost.

On reaching the bottom floor, she had contemplated escaping out the huge front doors to the garden. There were many places outside to hide; she knew them all from growing up on the Estate; knew every little nook and cranny where she could conceal herself or anything else she chose. But the age-effected hinges would reveal her presence there, which was why she had elected to hide in the passage instead, Paul's exit from the room above forcing her to take refuge behind the only cupboard. And now, if she just stayed still ...

The whites of her eyes prominent with fear, she knew she mustn't allow him to catch her. He must never find her. Yet now, he was only steps away. She could hear him breathing in the darkness. If she stayed motionless, if she made no sound that would give herself away, he might just go on past. Then she would run.

It was then the moon came out, its rays penetrating long fingers down the length of the hallway. Paul's shadow appeared beside her. Pressing back against the wall, Eva raised the knife high above her head. Just like the others who had stood to inherit a share of Gollen Manor, Paul Bennett didn't stand a chance.

∾

Any Place

You stand
red dusty clothes piled high in arms too young,
skinny legs straddling cracked verandah boards
as you stare across a Namatjira scene
where orange, ochre, golds sprawl to horizon's shimmer
punctuated only by glistening ghost gums
and dead dry gullies.

You listen
as a young crow plays with its language
strives for perfection in the lingering stillness
as you pad to the pump
The tumult of water pounding into battered buckets
transports you to crystal clear pools
where you frolic near thrumbling cascades
tumbling down a distant gorge
the sound takes you to any place but here.

You trip
barefoot to the copper
each muddy splatter conjures cloud filled skies
damp nardhu fields
and fat sleek brown cattle
as you plunge dusty moleskins, denim blue shirts, bandanas
scrub until the froth turns red,
the water liquid mud
then you dunk with disillusionment

Under an angry sun
you hang half people shapes
go back inside to burgeon your dreams with far distant places
places Grandpa painted in words
while you studied his face for the truth
but his face is like a roadmap of the places he's been,
each deep crevice swelling your mind with grand possibilities.

Outside the windmill sings –
like Dame Nellie Melba, grandpa says –
and you rush in desperation
shriek as a red cloud pirouettes the garden
jigs with faded moleskins;
jives with lazy shirt sleeves
waltzes along the fence that rolls forever.
Its howl bids you follow
invites you to places you've dreamt of
– to London
where ladies dress in fine lace and feathers
walk on needle heels
drink tea with elevated pinkies
talk in rounded vowels you sometimes practice.

Jostled by the wind swirl the crow flies off to a ghost gum
as you tear down your efforts
stomp inside and sweep the paddock from the table
fold red dusty clothes —
as you wish for black cockatoo skies,
a screeching Nellie Melba
mud pouring from the roof top
flooded nardhu fields
and market fat brown cattle
But all you hear is the mournful *Aaaaaah* from a treetop
And know it's the sound of lonely

A Time For Dawn

Death had little consequence for me until my eleventh year. It was a time when much of life was still to be experienced. I remember, though, when I was five, my Aunt Cecelia died and, for the first time in my life, I saw my father cry. I didn't know why.

One night a short while after her death, I'd asked him: "What's death, Daddy?"

We were sitting on the front porch of our Atlanta house after a late dinner. The sky was alive with glittering stars which made it hard to comprehend why my Dad was still so sad.

He placed his arms around his knees where he sat on the step and looked out across the yard. "Death is when someone stops living," he answered glumly. "They leave behind all those who are dear to them, and they go to live in Heaven."

"Is it painful?" I'd asked next.

"No. It's more painful for those who are left behind because it hurts your heart to lose someone you really love," he said.

It was my turn to stare idly across the vast, shadow-strewn, lawn. "Like when I lost Melissa when we moved to Nebraska?"

Father put his arm around my shoulders and drew me closer. "No," he'd laughed lightly. "You can still write to Melissa." He'd looked down at me. "When someone dies, Kitten, they are gone forever. You can't write to them, and you can't call them on the telephone. They're gone. Completely gone."

"Oh," I said, still not really understanding. "Is Heaven a nice place, Daddy?"

"I've heard so," he answered softly. Then he looked up at the sky. "Every one of those stars up there is someone who was once living here on earth," he said. "They stay up there looking down on us, making sure we are safe."

I too looked up. Heaven was immense.

"Aunt Celia is that big, bright star right there above Mr. Pateman's Pepper tree," he said, pointing to a particularly glittering star which seemed to shine brighter than the rest.

I hadn't known Aunt Cecelia at all for she lived in Seattle and we hadn't moved there yet, so I just said, "Oh."

I guess my Dad must have really loved Aunt Cecelia for her to be the biggest brightest star.

We weren't a very big family, that I could remember, and there weren't any more deaths for many years. There was, however, something which happened about five years later which prepared me well for my father's death in 1985.

We'd moved to Florida — we moved a lot when I was young. Father was an engineer on large building projects and Mother eventually dabbled in Real Estate. We had lived in Omaha, Nebraska, Georgia, Illinois and now in Juno Beach, Florida. We had a nice house about six blocks from the ocean in a quiet street lined with round topped trees. It would have been one of my favourite places in all the world, had I not met Dawn.

Dawn lived next door, yet I had been there for many weeks before I realised someone my age lived so close by. I'd given up making friends at school years earlier, realising that friends became too hard to leave behind when it was time to move again. I'd become a loner in a way - really, why bother making things, just to break them again, and friendships came fairly strongly into that category. My biggest wish at that time was to have a dog of my own, something for company, something that could walk with me, and sleep in my room; something I could talk to and take with us when we moved. But

Mom had said it wasn't fair to keep up-rooting a dog each time we moved, that is was hard for them to understand and find themselves new territories. I'd pondered that for a long while then wondered: What about me? Had they ever thought what it did to me?

Meeting Dawn was totally unintentional.

I'd been standing for some time at the end of the drive trying to decide what to do on that rather long Saturday when laughter caught my attention in the yard next door, followed by the sudden yapping of a dog. Peering around the bushes, I saw a girl, about my age, throwing a small yellow ball across the lawn to a dog. The dog was a reddish golden colour - almost the same as Mrs. Dantree's Persian ginger cat back in Idaho. It scampered down the path after the bouncing ball.

Immersed in their pleasure, I wandered along the pavement, sort of nonchalant like so I could watch them longer without being noticed.

Suddenly the yellow ball whizzed past my feet and rolled out into the roadway. A big red pickup was coming down the road towards the ball, and I gasped as the little golden pup skittered briskly after it, all yaps and ears flapping. Then I heard a scream. The girl was calling out for the dog to stop.

The red truck was closer, almost on top of the ball when I realised what was happening.

Stooping quickly, I scooped the reckless pup up into my arms and held tightly to its round squirming body. The truck's wheels caught the ball and sent it whizzing back towards us.

"Whoa," I said to the little dog. "Whoa! I'll get your ball."

The ball lay idle on the grass verge, so I picked it up and turned to hand it and the dog back to its rightful owner. But the girl still sat on the front lawn of her house, her hands covering her eyes, absolutely useless. She'd done nothing to save her dog, and therefore didn't deserve him. Angry, I strode up the path to where she sat.

"You could have tried to stop him!" I snapped accusingly.

The girl uncovered her eyes, and looked up. Large tears had spilled down her face. "Oh Goldy! Goldy!" she cried as she reached up for the puppy. "Oh thank you," she said. "Thank you."

I just shrugged. It had been nice to hold such a warm, cuddly dog as Goldy. He was beautiful, with large big brown eyes, and long, floppy, curly-haired ears. His body felt just so right in my hands. Short, squat and soft-bellied. His coat of orange was silken and long, and he had the cheekiest look on his face as his tongue lolled about in an effort to reach me.

Reluctantly I handed him down to her, my then empty hands going into the back pockets of my jeans. The girl made no move to rise, just took the dog and placed him in her lap. She kept looking up at me while the pup fussed and frolicked in an effort to lick her face.

There seemed no point just standing there, so I turned to leave. There had to be something I could do on a very dull Saturday.

"You're the new girl from next door, aren't you?" the girl asked.

I made a 'who-cares' face, and nodded. It seemed odd she knew about me but I hadn't known about her.

"I'm Dawn," she said brightly. "I'm so glad to meet you. And thank you for saving Goldy. I'm sure he would have been killed if you hadn't been there."

"Why didn't you stop him then?" I shot back pointedly. She was trying to be friendly, and I had to avoid making friends.

She looked glum. "I ... I can't walk at the moment," she answered apologetically.

The words took me back. Her legs looked alright, and I couldn't see a wheelchair anywhere.

"Why?" was all I could think to say, feeling stupid the instant I'd said it. It was really none of my business.

She looked more accepting. "I haven't been very well lately. Sometimes I have no strength or balance at all."

"Is that why I haven't seen you before?" I asked.

It was her turn to make a face then she nodded. "I've been in hospital for a while." Then she seemed to cast any thoughts to do with that aside. "What's your name?" she asked more brightly.

"I'm Bree," I told her. "Bree Williams."

"Hello Bree Williams. I've been dying to meet you."

She took me back again. Why ever would anyone want to meet me?! I looked her over.

She was dark haired, with large black-brown eyes framed heavily with lashes contained within a softly rounded face. She certainly looked healthy enough to me. Actually I thought she was very pretty, made more so by the dainty-looking dress which flounced out around her where she sat. I, on the other hand, was in a pair of faded blue denims with knees stained, patched from where I had fallen from, or worn out, fixing my bike. We seemed very different; and there was no way, even generously, I could call myself anything near pretty. I was plain; and very average. The only thing we might have had in common was our age. I didn't even have a dog.

"He's a beautiful dog," I noted, trying hard to muster the nerve to put this friendliness on hold. I wanted to tell her she would be the death of Goldy if she wasn't more careful, but instead I asked, "What kind is he?"

She scruffed his coat roughly as she smiled. "He's a cocker spaniel," she pronounced happily. "I got him for my birthday this year. Do you like him?"

I nodded, and mentioned glumly. "I've always wanted a dog."

It seemed the one thing we did have in common was our

growing love for that tiny, rebellious spaniel and I tried to tell myself for a long time the reason I kept going over to Dawn's was to visit with Goldy; that my pretending he was mine was the real reason our friendship grew.

In the months we lived at Juno Beach, Dawn became my truly best friend. We spent many days, once her illness went, walking along the beach front, or sitting up on the slopes overlooking the ocean. I sensed, however, as close as we became, there was something Dawn wasn't telling me. I also sensed it was something I didn't want to know.

One night, after Dawn had been away for several days, her parents drove us to the beach where they were going to stroll and indulge in a quiet coffee in one of the beachfront cafes. Dawn hadn't felt up to walking so we sat on the rocks where the waves washed gently in. The tide was going out, and gulls wafted on the breeze above the water, or sat idly in the moon-coloured blue. Goldy was sitting between us, his stumpy tail also idle with the mood Dawn was in. My arm was about his shoulders, Dawn's was around his rump, as we both looked out to sea.

"You do really love Goldy, don't you, Bree?" she suddenly stated without looking at me.

"Of course, I do," I answered back, almost with a laugh at the thoughts that sometimes crossed her mind. In fact I was terrified that one day my father would come home and say it was time to move again, for I would lose Dawn, and I would lose Goldy.

When Dawn remained silent for a long while, I looked across at her. She was always the one to lead the conversations, always chatting about this or that. But not tonight. Tonight, I saw the glistening of moisture on her cheeks, and, without due reason, it frightened me.

Then I heard her sniff, and swallow thickly, and she tried to inconspicuously wipe the tears from her face.

"What ..."

"I want you to have Goldy when I'm gone," she said suddenly, beating me to my question.

I frowned and looked at her with confusion. "What do you mean? Where ...?"

She sniffed again, but this time there were no tears accompanying it. "I'm dying, Bree. I want to know Goldy will be with someone who loves him when I'm gone. Mom and Dad never wanted a dog, but when I got sick, they gave me whatever I wanted. Please, say you'll take Goldy. I really only want you to have him."

She sniffed again.

Dumbstruck, I sat looking blankly at her, my mouth unable to move around the words I needed to ask, my eyes starting to burn and moisten all at the same time.

Then Dawn looked across at me as Goldy shot out between us and ran to chase the gulls from the beach. "I have a brain tumour," she said outright. "They can't stop it."

"Is that what's made you sick?"

She nodded. "We've known about it for a while now, but they thought they could fix it." She let out a loud sigh as if accepting what she had expected all along. "You will take Goldy, won't you? And you'll love him and care for him as much as I do?"

I reached over, wrapped my arms around her and hugged her tightly. I didn't want Dawn to go anywhere. I wanted Dawn to be my best friend for the rest of my life. I had finally found someone with whom I connected strongly, and now I was going to lose her. Tears burst from my eyes and my throat shut out the air.

"I'm so scared," I heard Dawn's muffled words in my ear. "I don't want to die."

Then we cried, arms locked around each other, and I felt a deep and lasting hollowness fill my soul so completely I thought I would stay empty for the rest of my life.

We had many months together before Dawn's illness took her. We spent long hours, and long nights, sitting on the beach, or on the rocks above the water, talking.

Somewhere along the way, Dawn accepted her fate, and returned to the bright soul I had first met. It was the fact that we had found each other that had made her dying seem so cruel. When it had just been her, she'd had little else to lose, except her parents who had also prepared themselves for the final inevitability.

The most lasting memory of my acceptance that death was indeed inevitable came on a night when the stars were full and brilliant, when they glittered like sparkling gems above us as we sat overlooking an emerald green sea dotted with satiated gulls. Dawn had known for just a short while that her days were short; that there would be no slow deterioration; no slow, fading illness. Her time would be sudden and quick and without warning. And she was ready.

We had talked a lot about death in the beginning then had avoided the subject completely, as if any mention of what was in the future would bring it on more quickly. We had become children - ignorant children playing children's games - disregarding the harsh realities life brought to us.

Yet this night, we were strangely silent. I knew Dawn was dwelling on what was to be; she had many silent moments now, more and more as the time drew nearer. I looked up and saw a particularly bright star shining just above the point further south.

"My Dad says that when you die you become a star so you can stay up there in Heaven and watch over us," I said, trying to sound wise and philosophical. "You could be that biggest, brightest star up there over the point, and you could watch out over me and Goldy."

Dawn remained silent a moment, looking up, looking at the biggest, brightest star I had found for her. Then her lips pursed tightly and she shook her head. "I don't want to be a star," she said frankly. "Stars only live in the darkest hours of night, and I want to be in the daylight, when it's at its brightest."

Dawn left us some weeks later, sleeping peacefully forever in the room above my bedroom window in the house next door. The comings and goings from her house alerted us to the tragedy unfolding, and Goldy, dashing around barking at the disturbance, was brought to my door. We sat, he and I, rugged warmly on the back porch looking eastward to the sea, hearing voices of men coming and going, as family members arrived to console Dawn's parents.

Goldy snuggled in against my side and I pretended Dawn was sitting on his other side as she usually did. I wondered if he knew we were losing something very dear to us. And, as the sky turned from ebony to violet-black to grey, as a warm golden hue arced brightly over the horizon, as it stretched its rays upward to brighten the lingering dark, when Dawn's mother cried out piteously with grief, I knew that Dawn had arisen, and that this was truly the time for Dawn.

&

Battle Beach – 6th of June.

The red, dead sea at Omaha
ebbs out, seeps in
litters lives upon the beach,
lingering lives,
lives fragmented
fear demented,
shaking, screaming,
praying
bob in surf, sit limp, stare lifeless.
Fish gag, shrapnel fins flap
as life ebbs out from the red washed sand
where life stains the land blood red.
Fish flip and flop like men
then airless, flop no more
drowned in guts
smothered in gore.

Bomb barrages
splatter the sand
their red display of target spray
drowns screams
shatters dreams.

Life shattered, splattered,
on the beach men tattered
sink heads to Tommy gun rattles
and they cry, Momma,
Momma, they cry.

"I don't like Omaha, Momma,"
the young child cries
as the soldier dies on the screen.
Before his face he's had a taste
of war.
He will play that game no more.

෴

Behind the Scenes

The music starts, the lights dim, the spotlight swings across the grass and up the castle wall. The entrance bars of music pierces the night, the arched doors open and out into the arena surges a big black charger, its black mane flying, astride it, the Captain of the Kings Troop Royal Horse Artillery in all his resplendent glory. Behind him gallops the Bugler, and behind him thunders the team of heavy blacks hauling the three-tonne gun. They peel to the right as the spotlight finds the finer team of browns hauling another gun. They peel to the left. The spotlight pulls back to flood the field with brilliance and colour. The Captain draws his sabre, holds it erect, barks an order, and the musical ride begins.

The crowd is transfixed, wincing as the teams haul the heavy guns around the field, mirroring movement, swinging them through wild loops and curves, then galloping the diagonals miss each other by inches, three tonnes of heavy gun ready to bring them down and take their souls if the timing isn't perfect. If one horse baulks the performance will be tragic.

We grimace behind the scenes, pray the gear holds, and ready ourselves for when the guns are disengaged and our teams gallop out to stand behind the grandstands out of sight. We leap into action, grabbing their bridles, keeping them from bolting as the cannons fire ceremonial retorts. On that cue we release and they gallop back to centre stage to retrieve the guns and surge back out of the arena. It seems only minutes since they left, since we released them for the very worrisome ride down Riverside Drive in the thick night traffic, to jog to the Esplanade for their grand and frightening entrance, these horses that are doing this for the very first time.

Soon they will be back for a costume change, the Kings Troop saddles and gun harness stripped, square high-backed saddles and velvet robes donned for the Knights of the Royal British Armoury. They will now have to endure the creak and crash of armour.

The ringing clash of metal on metal echoes round the enclosure as the horses are made ready, the two knights rehearsing the strokes they'll play in battle, then they double-check their carefully shaved lances and it is time. They mount, girths are tightened as they haul down their helmets, visors raised until the full-on joust. We step back and bid them well, and again pray the horses stay safe.

So how did we get here, standing behind the stands at Supreme Court Gardens, peeking out through centre stage entrance at a huge castle replica, complete with turrets and opening double arched gates? It started from a simple phone call asking for assistance. The Mounted Section of the State Emergency Service had been noted for its horsemanship and discipline at a recent riding display and our help was required by the organisors of the Perth International Tattoo. Being good little volunteers we jumped at the invitation to be involved.

This spectacular event would consist of the Kings Troop Royal Horse Artillery reproducing their world famous musical ride - a performance of 63 horses and ten three-tonne cannons - and a team of jousting knights to replicate the Days of Olde. Our role in this great plan was to find enough suitable horses and train them for the tasks in six months. And so we began.

The word went out and soon horses of all descriptions began arriving at the property allocated as the training centre. All were dark-coloured, a requirement of the Kings Troop. Ron, the Equestrian Coordinator, offered a couple of Friesians which he intended to showcase through the event. The difficulty was, Friesians were scarce in Perth, so, to aid his cause, two were imported from over east, one of them unbroken. Newly breaking a sizeable light draught horse and having it ready to perform in public under floodlights beside a percussion band in less than six months was impossible for the best of trainers, but, in the absence of an alternative, we started work.

Horses were trialled and *'binned'*, trialled and accepted, then trained for their role, which varied for some. The Friesians were the harness horses that would tow the three-tonne guns, and would also carry the armour-clad knights down a narrow lane of bunting while a jousting lance bore straight at them.

'Not a problem!'; we rolled our eyes.

But we only had four horses of one team, and the Kings Troop gun team had six. A millionaire's combined driving team, a kid's Pony Club horse and the unbroken gelding didn't even make one team, and the two part-bred, badly trained horses were far too dubious of character to risk the others. And we still needed a second team - and no more Friesians available. What else could we use for a gun team?

Ron said he knew of some standardbreds (*that's those trotting horses that race at Gloucester Park*) that worked as a carriage team in Kings Park. We could train them to tow a gun. Surely we could find two more!

Then we needed more horses for the Captain and the Bugler to ride. And the horses would also need to tent-peg because the Kings Troop had accepted an invitation to tent-peg against the WA Police Mounted Section. It was hair-tearing time – this handful of mismatched horses had to learn to tow the guns and accept the clash and clang of armour and having lances bearing down at their faces; they would never be able to tent-peg as well. We simply had to find more horses and fit them into our training programme. Did I mention anywhere that we were *volunteers?*

So in came more donations – horses for the causes, more testing and rejecting until a core group of horses looked half-way suitable. We began to mould and shape the horses in our charge, teaching the gun horses to work as a pair, the left horse ridden, the right hand horse led and obeying the bat. The bat is a small white stick with a loop each end, which is used to keep the led horse up with and close in against the left horse. This was all new to us too, never having ridden a carriage horse before, or used a bat. Next we worked them as a four, not yet harnessed together, selecting the staidest two as the wheel horses. This was Jordy, our Pony Club horse, and Grundgeon, would you believe, our newly broken gelding, who was accepting everything amazingly well.

Six months and a lot of dilemmas later, twenty-two horses were stabled up at Noalimba, the accommodation and training centre for the next month. Our international guests arrived shortly after – eight riders from the Kings Royal Horse Artillery, two Knights from the Royal British Armoury – all delightfully British lads who were eager to please and definitely determined to put on a cracking good show.

So the training, and hiccups, continued. The old World War II horse harnesses that were on loan for the performances were so decrepit they fell apart the first time used, almost pulling down the team - which was now an acceptable four - and the second team had not yet come to fruition. We explained to Ron what might happen when you hook four ex-racing standardbreds together and put them under floodlights in front of a crowd, but he just couldn't imagine it.

In due course, the riders became familiar with their mounts, the gun teams slowly became more settled, the jousting horses were less and less frightened by the lance and clang of the quintain, and we became quite proficient in centring that medieval device. The tent pegging horses were getting faster and faster and veered less and less from the white pegs in the ground. All was looking ready.

"Can you get me some big watermelons," the Captain asked one morning. "We might add in a sabre run to simulate beheadings."

So I go out and buy a half dozen watermelons and haul them back in a crate.

"What are they?" asks the Captain.

"Watermelons," say I.

"But I only want them about this big." He indicates the size of a rockmelon.

"This is the smallest they had," say I. So daily we cut them in half and stuck them on the sticks. You just wouldn't get a ripe watermelon small as that.

Dress rehearsal came and looked magnificent, the only problem was the Captain couldn't see with his busby on; was totally blind, which apparently was common. They remedied this by the Bugler calling out instructions: "Go faster, Sir. Go slower, Sir. Halt there, Sir."

So here we were on the grounds at Supreme Court Gardens, twenty-two barely trained horses, a riding-blind Captain, a brand new set of harness per team, made through the nights by a bleary-eyed Kings Troop Saddler and a local saddlemaker, a team of Friesian horses hooked together and extremely touchy, a team of four standardbreds just waiting for the lights and music to race each other, a team of ten partly trained tent-peggers, and our rabbly group acting as backstage grooms, squires and crash team dummies ready to leap to the cause to save a horse or rider – with strict instructions: "Don't cut off my armour! It's terribly expensive."

We had vets and chiropractors on hand for any mishap, and a good supply of Rescue Remedy with which we liberally laced the horses (and some riders) before sending them out the gates and down the road to Riverside Drive, the bright sparkling lights of heavy traffic showing only silhouettes of two teams of magnificent horses towing two three-tonne cannons like professionals.

In those quiet moments, shattered only by the clashing of one broad sword against another in the background, I wondered if the crowd in the stands had any inkling of the effort and challenges suffered and overcome by a handful of dedicated people to bring this spectacle together, that, as the castle doors swung open and in charged the blind Captain of the Troop, big black Mandy veering with fright all the way down the centre of the arena with the Bugler saying: "Left Sir. Right, Sir. More Right, Sir. Halt, Sir," in amongst that gun team was Grundgeon, wheel horse extra-ordinaire, undaunted jousting horse of the callous Black Knight. Our newly broken gelding had taken up the challenge and learnt as much as we had, performing to a level of excellence night after breath-taking night.

By the end of the week, with memories stored for a life-time, we agreed whole-heartedly with the White Knight: We all had a cracking good time.

And mine will be the first hand up if they ever do it again.

₧

Brave Molly

The steady plod of solid feet upon the distant sands
where soldiers rest upon their seats, mates guided by their hands
across their backs their rifles slung, not needed at this time
They stand to face the enemy's gun, wait for orders down the line.

And then it comes, "Fall into line!" they swing to line abreast
their horses champing on the wire, this charge will be the test.
For who will hold their courage, their line held on the run
and who will beat the barrage, and charge beneath the guns.

"Fix bayonets!" comes the call now, metal clinks as this is done,
and now the horses stand there, manes tossing in the sun.
Chestnuts, browns, a dun or two, each tired from the sands,
from walking endless hours to make this final stand.

For water now they're desperate and it spreads beyond the guns,
their life hangs in the balance and for this they make their run.
The captain gives the order and the riders ease the rein,
the horses all move forward, not one of them detained.

They march as one along the sand, picking up the pace,
till Captain shouts the order that starts this final race.
Sand kicks up from the desert, a dust cloud rising high
as the horses gallop freely, to succeed or else to die.

Across the burning desert sands, the soldiers make their run.
The horses bravely galloping, their coats reflecting sun
as bullets whiz and plop around destroying targets large,
as soldiers duck their heads and yell on the Tenth Light Horse last charge

Mick was riding on the flank, his Molly in full flight.
His hands were trembling on the reins when he felt the bullets bite.
The impact knocked him from his horse with a loud resounding whack;
he hit the sand, lay deathly still till Molly trotted back.

She stood with him beneath the sun as the battle raged around,
her body casting shadows over Mick upon the ground.
At times she gently nuzzled him in asking him to rise.
And Mick looked up and blessed her - to him she was a prize.

He'd picked her out some months ago, this roguish chestnut mare,
so wild of eye, she'd challenged him to 'ride me if you dare'.
They had some fights, some breaking of the man, the horse and saddles.
Till one day she'd agreeably let Mick stay full a-straddle.

Until that time had happened her strength and courage bound
meant sometimes Mick was mounted, the next upon the ground.
Yet something 'bout this chestnut mare, in his heart she held the place,
'tis where he kept those cherished things, now his fingers stroked her face.

She nickered soft and deeply as her muzzle touched his cheek
as she tried to push him upward but he was quickly growing weak
for the bullets passed right through him
                              and his head was pained and addled
But Molly lay beside him to help him in the saddle.

"Good on you, mate," he told her as he barely swung astride
"We may have had our differences but, girl, you've done me proud,"
And up she stood with Mick aboard and gentle made her tread
back to the line from whence she came, too late though – Mick was dead.

But Molly Girl was treasured for the role she played that day
in bringing home her Hero from the sand where he had lay
A part of war-time history, the Tenth Light Horse last run
when they charged through hails of bullets in the desert 'neath the sun.

&

Crocs on the Highway

'Lake Mackay is full and overflowing, flood damaging the roads. Kiwirrkurra, for the second time in three years, has had a lot of rain. Previously, no rain has fallen for over eight years. The population is 130, plus administration staff. The Aboriginal community will be okay provided there is no more rain.

Five houses in the lower lying areas have been evacuated. Water is running down either side of the airstrip, filling up a small lake that has developed at its end. Water is creeping into the community. Septics are seeping. Toilets are not flushing. Vehicles are getting bogged right throughout the community, isolating residents.

All roads into Kiwirrkurra are impassable due to the high water table.

Alice Springs to Kintore, Northern Territory, may be accessible in two to three weeks.

Kintore, Northern Territory to Kiwirrkurra, Western Australia will be impassable for another four to six weeks, depending on the weather.

The road from Western Australia is impassable and may be so for three to four weeks.

All roads in this area are desert tracks.'

This was a partial report on the aftermath of Cyclone Steve. Some areas were far worse. In some instances arrangements were made for Health Department officials to fly in to some communities and assess the health risks, with an official accompanying them to eradicate dogs.

"Hey, there's a croc up on the highway," Mick said as I read over the report. "Big bugger. Nearly hit him driving in." He drops his scruffy, orange peak cap on my desk.

Out on the tarmac of Broome Airport, two Caribou aircraft squat as flight crews from the Royal Australian Air Force await their next round of orders. The aircraft look big bellied and cumbersome compared to the Hercules C130 parked behind them, *The Stallion 094* crew also awaiting orders.

Unlike the Caribou, the Herc's belly is impregnated with parachutes, enormous khaki silks on thick bands of webbing, each costing $8,000.00. On them will float down pallets of well-trussed drums of fuel, four 200 litre drums to a pallet. Other pallets will follow, containing essential items. Meat, vegetables, fruit, dry goods, powdered milk, toiletries, babies needs. No ice-cream, no soft drinks, no cigarettes. Barramundi however is approved as it is part of the community's staple diet. Smoked oysters are not, and are retrieved from their hiding place in the bins.

Our organisation's responsibility is to ensure that only essential goods are sent, for the bill is astronomical.

As a volunteer of the State Emergency Service I assist in prolonged operations such as these. As a long term, experienced volunteer I sometimes get perks. This short-notice trip to Broome is one of them. Usually during disasters I sit in the underground bunker in Perth, tracking cyclones, and arranging resources and manpower to send to affected areas. This time I am the resource. My experience with cyclones is well documented: all done on paper. So this is all new to me.

As we flew across the country, heading north, I was astounded at the massive change in the landscape. The Great Sandy Desert was awash and dotted with flocks of pelicans. *Pelicans? Inland?* Roads that normally stretched for hundreds of miles, their laser straightness slicing the country below, are partly hidden, cut by water. The surrounding desert is green – in many places blue as mile-wide lakes abound.

This was Steve's effect.

At this time of year, there is no rest in the tropics, and Rosita came gusting in unpredictably hard and fast on his tail. A Category Four cyclone. Not quite as severe as Vance that demolished Exmouth, but strong enough to give the town a thorough whacking.

Broome itself suffered little structural damage – six houses in all requiring roof repair, and not much else. Power went out, but the quaint simulated-corrugated iron abodes stood the force of nature's wrath well, unlike the luxuriant growth of tropical palms and vegetation. Everything was shredded. Rows of stringy fronds and dead dry branches pile above head height, lining verges like hedgerows – the gathered result of chainsaw crews flown in from across the State. In some streets Shire trucks and front-end loaders dismantle the hedge rows, loading them onto trucks that ship them out of town for mulching or burning. It will take months to clear the debris.

Trees, still standing, lay at precarious angles to the ground. Some have their tops ripped out and will probably die later. This will prolong the clean up. Feelings of devastation in the town will soon develop as the realisation of a long restoration grows more apparent. The clean up itself will take only months, the time needed to restore nature to its best will take many years.

Outside my office window council workers move the pink Broome sand from the car park with a blower, ejecting it to nowhere. The dust billows in the hot humid air, coating mud-splattered four wheel drives that line the curb. They have just brought in the SES crews for lunch, the crews that have been chain-sawing dangerous branches and palm trees that still teeter over houses and roads. They have come a long way. Kunnanurra. Gosnells. Belmont. Port

Hedland. Newman. Perth.

Members from the Bunbury region aid the RAAF. They are the lucky ones, flying out to isolated airstrips in Cessnas to retrieve and repack the giant chutes and return them to the Hercules for subsequent trips. The SES boys eat while the Hercules crew waits for the field engineer who has been touring the outlying airstrips, assessing them for landing suitability. On his appraisal, the decision is made to use the Hercules or the two Caribou, and whether to land and off-load or drop the goods through the air.

"What are we going to do about that croc up on the Highway?" Mick asks, coming back into the office. Mick is the Aboriginal Liaison Officer from Big Water: Kunnanurra. An indigenous tracker, he is heavily bearded and of Irish descent.

"It's not our problem," I say, "but I'll phone the Ranger so he can deal with it."

"Ranger's herding that big'un that was hanging round the old harbour back down the coast."

"I suppose I should phone the Police then," I guess with a shrug.

Mick nods. "Just hope no-one's dumb enough to get out of their car to shoo it off the road."

We look at each other, wary. *Would a tourist be so stupid?* I immediately snatch up the phone.

Eventually, the chainsaw crews return to the 32 degree heat and humidity outside. In Perth it is raining, and I had packed only winter clothes for the trip. My uniform is summer weight so I am lucky, though I will duck into town to buy some casuals later.

In the mid afternoon, the RAAF come in. After a few phone calls to Canberra they recommence the resupply runs – if the

Hercules will start. And a tyre has developed a hole in it and will soon need changing. Roy, their Liaison Officer, keeps glancing at my shoulder stripes as we talk. I outrank him for, in his organisation, my three stripes is a Wing Commander. He only wears a stripe and a half. Though worlds apart, our organisation's ranking system was designed on the military's, so I have his respect.

The afternoon drops are organised. Fuel for Ringer Soak, Yakannara, Yagga Yagga. Returned evacuees from Bidjidanga need food. So do the communities of Kumbrarumba, Biljidlbidi, Purnawala, Ngarantjadu ('With a silent G,' Mick says) and Nookanbah. Tons of food. Tons of fuel. Only a few airstrips can take the Herc. The Caribou needs only six hundred metres to land and a hundred metres to take off, so is loaded with supplies. Pallets of essential stuff. The two Caribou carry the load of one Herc, which will do an air drop elsewhere. The RAAF boys head back to the Airport.

Their planes are impressive on the tarmac, catching the eye of the endless line of tourists pouring in and out of the facility. Though interested, the holidayers show little concern that a cyclone has savaged the town. As long as the flat cream sand of Cable Beach is accessible that is all that matters.

We continue to organise flights. Balgo is running low on everything. They will have to wait till tomorrow as a Hercules is flying in from Canberra in the late afternoon to change the faulty tyre. RAAF RAC, we joke. In the interim, I head out, to try to find where I can buy a *West Australian*. There is precious little time for sight-seeing on this rigorous duty so I see what I can of the sights on these daily hunting trips.

"Avoid the highway," Mick warns as I leave. "And watch your back."

Frowning, I find my hire car in the car park – this place is very strange.

At first sight, Broome is a small quaint tourist town, its array of tanned nationalities belong to its history. Japanese. Chinese. European. Polynesian. Aboriginal. They all live in harmony. The town is clean, apart from Rosita's rubble, which is quickly forgiven. The tide is in at this hour, and for the first time I see the far distant emerald stretching to the shore, its shades gently lifting till cyan ripples in amongst the mangroves. Boats, which normally anchor well out of reach of the 25 foot tide, now bob on taut ropes amongst the mangroves, metres from land.

Skirting town, I enjoy the dazzling green. Waves wash white and frothy against the rocks of a new apartment complex built upon the shore. Last night's meeting tagged it a high risk location as it is well within range of the expected four to five metre storm surge. The place might go under in the next big blow. The premises are listed for priority evacuation in the next big storm.

I pass a park bordered by road and mangroves. Something big is moving up the slope from the water, moving slow and lethargic. Really big. I u-turn swiftly and head back to the office, and within minutes am back on the phone.

"Has anyone moved that croc off the highway yet?" I ask the Police. "If you did, I think it's moved on to the park down near the Catalinas."

"No, not yet," comes the reply. "We're directing traffic round it at the moment. It doesn't seem to want to move."

"Well we have another big problem then," I tell him.

When Mick comes in I tell him the problem too.

"I told you to watch your back," he says. "They're coming in everywhere. RAAF crew seen lots of them buggers well inland. Laying on creek banks, all lined up one next to another. Storm has blown them in. I told you to keep your eye open or they'll sneak in up behind you. And that big croc's still laying up on the highway."

We flew back to Perth a few long days later. With resupply to the communities completed at least for the next few weeks; with the RAAF boys re-stationed to Telfa to resupply the Pilbara; with the croc now safely dispatched off the road, of his own blessed accord, I looked longingly down at the ocean as the plane angled skyward. The stunning iridescent green spread, white streaked. I'd had no time to use it. The long cream strip of unadulterated sand dotted with tourists. I'd had no time to walk on it.

Just off shore, amazingly visible in the clear blue-green were two floating lines. I pointed them out to my Supervisor beside me.

"Crocs," he said knowingly. "Looks like they're heading for Cable Beach."

Beautiful Cable Beach. I kept a watch on the crocs as they advanced to the point, remembering my week-long stay at the beautiful Palms Resort, my free air flight from and to Perth and the wonderful experience of helping with the restoration of Broome.

"Cable Beach, ay?" I say, smiling as one eyebrow hikes.

Tourists below bob and frolic in the surf where I once had really wanted to be. "Gee, right now I really love being a homeward bound volunteer."

Tourists in town

Minor Damage at Cable Beach Resort

Cable Beach lost some of its sand in places.

Devachan
(Place of the Gods)

Speak ye all in whispers at the death-side of the bed
for seeming gone to mortal life thoughts ripple through his head
as quietly he dwells on life and of his lessons learned,
the wrongs, the rights, what counted, the credits he has earned.
The silver cord is stretching, thin, death passes with a sigh.
The thread of life is fraying to the ladder to the skies.
The climb begins in earnest as reflections gold cast true
and influence what lies ahead, a future formed anew.

Speak ye all in whispers while at bardo's door he stands
met by friends and loved ones, who instant take his hand
and lead him to the hinterworld, the world of peace and light
where in repose he ruminates on all the things done right;
and shedding off the robes of earth, the fabric now outworn
he starts a new progression, has not died but been reborn.
He spends a time in Devachan, and plans his life anew,
writes his new born destiny, more credits to accrue.

And so I speak in whispers and hold his lifeless hand
that I might still stay close to him, that I might hear his plan
so we might be together in another place and time,
our futures then will be the same, linked in love, sublime.
For in this life immortal we will one day meet again
maybe not in Devachan but on an earthly plane.
The silver cord is severed, his golden soul lifts high
I hold a sob and smile, and kiss him soft, goodbye.

❧

From a Blanket

Sunset on the water,
fire in the sky,
the lake's black onyx surface
mirrors birds a-winging by.
The gentle hush of nightfall
as purple hues now blaze
to end the joyful light that's shared
in loving summer days.
But with the coming of the night
so too does come the time
for quiet, soft caresses
and body's endless rhyme.
And locked in love
the dawn will pend
horizons black, now gold,
sunrise on the water now
just as glorious to behold.

From the Steps of Bradley Street

Old and wizen, he sat on the steps of the tenement house on Bradley Street, his tired lungs panting to take in more air. Glancing back over his shoulder at the drab grey-stone building, in particular at the dingy flight of stairs that ascended to his first floor apartment, he eased his laboured breathing and pondered the stairs just a little longer. It was as arduous coming down now as it was to clamber up, he realised bleakly, momentarily considering a move to the lower level. But it was only a glint of a thought – he couldn't possibly give up Number Ten; couldn't bear the thought of leaving all those memories … and at his time of life, memories were all he had. Memories and Number Ten -- for inside Number Ten, Sophie Jessop still lived.

'No,' he discounted the thought. He could suffer the long climb up and down; could suffer it as long as his precious Sophie stayed vibrant in his heart.

His breathing back to normal, he pushed his ancient body upward off the step, felt the nagging twinge vice sharply in his chest - just for a second - a stern reminder to reconsider his original thought.

Instead, however, he contemplated the chances of joining the one he so constantly missed. It wouldn't be so bad, he huffed breathlessly at the pain. Living. Dying. Neither mattered much. Either way, he would do it alone. Death would be a peaceful release to his life, and nobody would miss him much.

He rubbed his chest absently till the twinge was gone, and pushed the thought of dying to follow it. Apparently it would not be today. And that was good, he mused. It was a nice day. The sun was shining.

And the sun was shining. It poked its rays between the high-rise city buildings to the east, creeping fingers of warmth over Bradley Street. The old man's head turned left then right. The park would make a pleasant stroll today, he decided languidly.

He lowered his foot down the step, gripped a weathered hand on the newel to support his slender frame. He let his other foot join the first, sliding and clutching his hand along the concrete railing as he did. Repeating the process two … three times, he finally came to rest on the square-slabbed walk below the porch.

There he looked out across the pavement, his beagle-hound eyes wide, depthlessly brown, and blinking with a youthful light that belied his preoccupation with death. Not that he was afraid of dying – he wasn't. He was ready for it when it came. Old men usually were. But it wouldn't be today … it was a nice day, he repeated silently with a nod.

He stood a moment, stooped in his usual fashion, feeling the gentle gusts ruffle the shock of white that capped his head in generous profusion. His broad, flat nose wrinkled as odours of rotting fruit and overflowing garbage bins long overdue for removal, wafted to it on the breeze. The furrows of his face creased further, the stench displeasing his senses.

The acrimonious stink was enough to start him moving.

He shuffled his feet to point northward, the direction of Hudson Park, and prepared to walk on buckled legs that were these days becoming far more difficult to control. For this slight flaw to his mobility he used a cane, a polished brown cane, heavily knuckled with stunted nodes that denoted its previous life. He used it now in his left hand and steadied his stance.

Straightening as best he could, he started the feet shuffling forward. That was when he noticed her on the steps of the Rosa Building adjoining, a building much the same as the one he had just descended. His eyes brightened instantly and he smiled, though it could not be fully seen. His heavily bristled top lip concealed much of the glad expression, but the grooves that masked the corners of his hidden mouth deepened and widened. His eyes said the rest. He raised an open hand in waving and shambled forward.

"Good morning to you, Mrs Haslop," he said, his mood now brighter, his voice cheery but husky with effort.

"Good morning, Mr Jessop," said she, feeling less depressed with the world in the old man's presence. Mr Jessop had a way of making people smile, she reflected, inwardly debating whether it was infectious or habitual. She certainly hadn't felt like smiling that morning.

"And where be you off to?" she asked, a mixture of nosiness and concern for his ailing health.

He ran a pointed finger across a thick forest of eyebrow, snow-capped to match his hair and lip cover. It was then the assimilation occurred to her of his blizzard-like appearance – white from snow, huddled as from cold, creviced features from blustery gelid winds. The look did not befit the climate of Southern California … but then, he hadn't lived here all his life, had he? she mused.

No. Fifteen years at the Sampson House next door, he had once told her. Thirty years in Washington, as a businessman – he had owned a grocery store. They had moved west to warmer climes for Sophie Jessop's health, which had bought her ten more years … ten very happy years. Before that, as a much younger man, he had escaped death at Treblinka II. Brave and determined, he had rebelled, and survived, and with the same qualities he had found America and a loving Jewish wife.

It had been a very sad story, with a happy middle. It would have a very sad end. His body and face now bore the scars of the hard life he had endured. But he raised another smile, and so did she. If he could, she thought, most certainly she could.

"Hudson Park," he answered, his finger still scratching thoughtfully at the forest. "The pigeons will be waiting today," he chuckled. "It's a beautiful day, Mrs Haslop …"

He had reached the bottom step and, stooped, was looking up as best he could. "… why waste it on sweeping the porch? Come with me," he beckoned. He bore down on the cane even harder with his other hand.

Leaning the dilapidated broom against the doorway, she dusted grimy hands on the apron that protected her pink floral day frock. She could see the garbage truck entering the far end of the street, the bang and rattle of bins promising more acceptable breezes. Dearly she would have liked to accept his offer but there was much she still had to do inside.

She called back down the step, shouting to be heard above the din of crashing metal. "Not today, Mr Jessop," she grinned. "Besides, my Harvey would have a screaming fit if I go running off all day with a younger man."

"Go on with you, Mrs Haslop. You make an old man's day," he chuckled, then continued to shuffle on. "I'll enjoy it for us both." His right hand waved, a downward backward motion as his back dominated.

She stood and watched a while longer as his eight-decade frame put distance slowly between them. It was becoming blatantly obvious his body was aging much faster these days, his steps becoming slower, the rest stops much longer. And that made her sad again. She wondered from her porch, where was his son? She knew he had one – he had told her years ago. Leo Jessop had a wonderful son. Somewhere in Washington, he said. George Lennard Jessop was his name.

A cold shiver ran the length of her spine. She knew she would be contacting George before the fall.

Picking up the broom again, she shot a quick glance down the street. Mr Jessop was at the corner, holding up the street pole. His other hand pressed hard down on the cane. When the traffic stopped he scuffed his feet onward across the intersection.

The pigeons were waiting.

&

hoops

You
train me
to jump through hoops
wear flowers in my aura
flaunt feathers and finery
to lift the eyes from tattered skirts
you dress me in

I
spin within your hoops
camouflage my thoughts with joyful smiles
wear purple warmers on my wrists
to hide the scars
caused by your eternal domination

You
spruik to crowds
who watch my daily act
watch me spinning in your rule
gyrating to your constant requirements
as I lose my identity
in an ocean of regret
and fix the smile rigid
to hide the thoughts within

I
founder
torn between first love and marital duty
wrestle with a pride too long suppressed
and try to stay afloat
knowing that all you see
is the size of the ring that binds me
never knowing that ...

You
are the hole in my boat
and
I
drown
'neath the weight of your expectations

&

In Bradley's House

She walked down the street carrying only her long grey shoulder bag, the tattered fabric matching her long loose trousers and long-sleeved, thigh-length overshirt. Her drab green floppy hat was pulled down over dark brown eyes, over long dark hair that she had, as usual, pushed crudely up inside to hide its beauty and protect it from the harsh rays of sunlight beating down upon her back. She walked silently, retracing the steps she'd often walked from the town in the late afternoon, the limestone edges almost rutted by her single path. Su-Lin's path, Brad had called it.

She pushed the thought away. She did not want to think of Brad right now. Now was not the time.

Moving further off the road as a black car swept by, she turned her head to avoid the swirl of dust and litter; kept her head turned until the car disappeared round the bend. She tried not to think about where it was going. It would make little difference.

Soon enough she reached the curve and far across the pasture saw the house, a house with many windows, its two-storied elegance nestled in the cove of towering magnolias where one summer they had erected the garden swing.

The fields were deep in grass, the tips browning slightly with the season, the surrounding fences standing crooked with neglect. She reached the driveway, its edges overgrown by red Bergia and dog-rose, the house sulking at its abandonment, its boards chipped and shedding the white coat Brad had lathered on it. The purple wisteria that had trailed across the balconies and ornate latticework were now skeletal – and she thought about Brad again, and pushed the thought away.

Ignoring the three black cars parked out front, she followed the drive to the back of the house, stepped up on the wide slatted verandah and entered through the open back door.

Inwardly she smiled — he had not put up curtains in her kitchen even though he had often threatened to. Maybe he too liked to look out the window and remember what she remembered, the freshly mown fields spreading out like rice paddies, each paddock coloured different by the separate days of mowing, each looking like terraces of paddies on the mountains of her home. Some days they made her sad and she longed for the palm trees and the umbrage of jungle growth around it. Some days she couldn't wait for the fields to grow and hide her long term memories. Those days she wanted to hang curtains and hide the view in total.

But not today. Today the curtain-less windows meant so much to her.

She turned and faced the kitchen, a large room bordered by many cupboards — cream cupboards in a pale green room — a bright room now buried in dust and leaves. Had no-one shut the door in all that time?

She heard footsteps on the stairway coming down, clunking hollowly as they always did, and voices carried in the next room. She pulled the hat from her head, shook the tresses loose and laid her bag and hat on the huge wooden table, not bothering to sweep it clean. She would have enough time for that much later.

A light flicked on in the next room, its glow shining through the gap beneath the swinging door. A shadow crossed the room, and she turned her back on it and opened the refrigerator. Every shelf was choked with ice, its solid crystal whiteness binding every metal tray to the next, and in amongst it she thought she could see a beer can. Brad liked his beer cold. She noticed too the open can of dog food just within the frozen boundaries of the lower shelf, and that was all.

She wondered if Maska was even known of.

She turned to the table, pulled out the three pies and an apple she had purchased in the town, the voices becoming louder as she unwrapped two pies.

From the cupboard she took the old chipped plate, set one pie upon it, placed the plate on the edge of the verandah. Pulling a few large leaves from the magnolia tree, she set the other pie across them, decorated the leaves with a few carefully placed blooms from the garden and a quarter of the apple and placed it as an offering on the grass beside the step; she knelt and bowed fully. Rising to her knees again, she looked up as a shadow cast across her.

A man stood on the verandah, staring sternly down, his face surprisingly familiar, maybe even handsome if he did not scowl so much. She rose to her feet, bowed slightly then, the customary pleasantries dealt with, said:

"I Suey-Lin. This my house. You go now."

The man's scowl was replaced by wide-eyed rage, no sign of surprise at her presence. "No! This is my brother's house! *You* have no right being here."

She shook her head, her long hair swaying with defiance. "I no leave. My house," she insisted as she climbed the steps.

A woman stepped out to stand behind the man and Su-Lin brushed passed her. Two more men standing in the kitchen moved aside as she entered.

"You all go now. You no belong here."

The man stormed in after her. "If you don't leave now I'll have you thrown out," he bellowed at her back.

Su-Lin, her head bent, pulled the broom from the cupboard and began to sweep the floor.

"Did you hear me?" he bellowed again.

She heard the woman's voice, saw her ease the man back to the doorway. "John, leave this to me. I'll talk to her. Go on out, all of you."

Su-Lin felt relieved that the anger in the room had gone. The offering for peace and prosperity on the doorstep was working again. She kept sweeping.

"Su-Lin, stop," the woman said. "We need to talk."

Su-Lin looked at her. "This my house," she reiterated firmly. "Su-Lin live here long time."

"I know. But you left here. You left Bradley and went home. This house belongs to Bradley's estate and will go to his family."

"I Bradley's family," she said softly. "Bradley say this Su-Lin's house. This Suey-Lin's kitchen. Suey-Lin's verandah. Suey-Lin come back now."

"But you left him. You are no longer entitled."

For the first time tears touched her eyes and she looked straight at the woman. "I no leave Bradley! Mr Winston call Bradley home. Say 'You come home now and no bring that whore. I no whore. I Bradley's wife." She started to whisk the leaves from the table. "I wait long time for Bradley come home. He come for short time then go again. He change. He very different. Then he send me home. I no understand but I go. He very different."

"Bradley was sick, Su-Lin," the woman said. "He got sick in the war and needed his family to look after him."

Su-Lin was silent. She knew the things that happened in the war; she knew the devastation on the men who'd fought on both sides, the devastation on the land. She had met Bradley in Long Dat before the last assault and spent time with him in her village while the damage was repaired. He had promised her they would make a life in America. He would get them a nice little farm where she could grow her vegetables and work the fields to her heart's content. He had brought her here and they had shared their lives, for years - until his father called him home. Then, after his last visit, he'd sent her back to her village high up in the mountains.

Then the letter came. He was very ill - he needed her to take over his affairs, to take over the farm, their farm, and if the worst happened before she arrived, her farm. She had used the ticket he had sent and returned, praying she would be in time.

"War a very bad thing," she said. "War in your family very bad too."

The woman looked sympathetic. "I know," she said. "They are rich and don't like outsiders. Even I have trouble fitting in. But I know they won't let you keep this place. They'll fight you every step of the way."

"They fight all they like. Su-Lin live here in Bradley's house. Bradley say I stay. Su-Lin have letter."

"They'll fight you with lawyers. You have no chance of winning, Su-Lin. Just leave now and save yourself a lot of heartache and money, money they know you don't have."

"Su-Lin have money. Bradley sent much money."

Footsteps on the verandah turned her head and a moment later the angry man strode back through the doorway. "Okay, I've had enough! You, get your bag and get the hell off this property. I've called our lawyer and he's preparing documents to bar you from being here. You have no right to this property whatsoever, regardless what you think."

Su-Lin flicked a glare back at him.

"John, Su-Lin is Bradley's wife. They were married."

The man snorted. "No pathetic marriage service held in a pox-ridden village in a war zone is going to hold up in any court of law. Where is the paperwork? It could be just what she says ... Brad wouldn't in a blue fit ..."

"We marry here in America too," Su-Lin said as calmly as her temper allowed.

The man slapped his forehead with the heel of his hand. "Damn him. How bloody stupid could he be?!"

"Bradley good man," Su-Lin defended. "Not coward like brother. Honest man. Made good husband. Would have made good father."

Myriads of moments of her life with Brad flicked through her mind, moments she would treasure to the end of her days. Moments too she had envisaged of the future, the whole family playing together, laughing under the magnolias.

The woman turned to her, frowning. "What do you mean?"

"Su-Lin heavy with Bradley's child when he send Su-Lin back to village. Say he no want son to see him with sickness. Want his son to grow up strong and good like people in my village; not want son damaged by Winston family. Better off alone he say. Su-Lin see how angry Bradley is with family. He not want go home - only went because he sick. Bradley love Su-Lin and Kai. Not want leave us alone. We go on now without Bradley."

She saw the redness grow on the brother's face and hid the pain from hers; looked up as a familiar scratching came from the verandah. "Maska?" she cried. "Maska?"

A tall wiry deerhound appeared in the doorway, its tail wagging its whole grey body. "Oh Maska!" Tears fell freely now.

She had felt so alone for so-so long. Leaving Kai with friends until she was settled was heartbreaking, leaving Maska, the wonderful dog Bradley had given her as a pup, behind when she left for Vietnam was devastating. But losing Brad had destroyed her soul completely. But the farm, Kai and Maska could restore it for all were part of him.

She straightened her back as the dog bounded towards her, felt the life coming back into her soul; her family evolving; she could see them all laughing beneath the magnolias for Brad would always be here in this place with her.

"You go now," she said to them all, unafraid of future consequences. The offering on the verandah was working fully, working strong, all good things coming back into her life. "You fight me however long you want, but you not come here again. This my place. This Bradley house. Bradley house where I belong."

She knew, standing beneath those grand magnolia trees with Maska leaning gently against her thigh on one side and the faint sense of Bradley on her other, watching them drive away that they would never return to destroy the dream she and Brad created. Her family would grow strong, and she would grow whole again in Bradley's house.

∾

Island Time

Christmas Island is a rare and hidden beauty, a paradise in the middle of the ocean. It moves with a slow and gentle grace that can only be appreciated from experience.

We flew to the island on a Friday in early November, hopping across the ocean from Learmonth to Cocos Island then on to the third most dangerous airport in the world. Sheer cliffs border the tarmac, rising up on our left to another plateau, dropping down into the ocean on the right, leaving no room for human error. Any mistake splatters you across the cliff-face or drops you into the drink. There is no radar on Christmas Island so landing is attempted only with clear visibility. Any fog and the plane diverts to Jakarta. We will be here for a week, there being one flight in and out, on Fridays. Empty seats on the plane are loaded with precious food, and trucks lumber along the tarmac to collect the island's supplies.

We are here to deliver Cliff Rescue training to the Islanders, an intensive four day course which leaves us three days free to explore the jungles and coastlines. Hire vehicles are waiting at the airport and we stow our luggage, toeing aside a few red crabs playing Customs with our bags before heading for the VQ3 Lodge down in The Settlement. November is the start of the red crab migration so, driving down the steep mountain road, we not only have to watch out for other traffic but also have to dodge every red pedestrian crab. If seen driving without due regard to crabs, Parks and Gardens officers confiscate the car.

Crabs on the road come in two varieties: runners and squatters. Those that squat usually survive. Runners become an easy feed for the massive population of feral cats.

Christmas Island is layered in five plateaus, the first beneath the ocean so everywhere you travel away from the coast you take the mountain road. This curves back and forth around tall cliff walls as it heads up the mountain - one lane up, one lane down, the lanes divided by a double white line. In crab migration season these lines are disregarded, only applying to oncoming traffic when no crabs hamper forward movement, otherwise you veer anywhere you like to avoid crunching tiny little bodies under the wheels. The migration occurs at breeding time when the crabs sidle out of the jungle and trek down the mountain to the coast. Reaching the sea, they perform a comical, ritualistic dance, lay their eggs, and crab-walk back to the jungle. On many roads low plastic buffer guards channel the flow of crabs away from the road, but when the full onslaught is on, these are useless and most roads on the island are closed.

We reach our lodgings and soon realise crabs are everywhere; they even climb the steps to our quarters. Thankfully they are timid creatures that scurry out of the way though I did during an idle moment encounter a cluster hell-bent on untying my shoelaces.

The weather on Christmas Island is warm and humid, the hotel room air-conditioned and meeting our basic needs. VQ3 is a friendly place where lodgers sit and chat on balconies and look out onto lava rock-faces, which are also daubed with … red crabs. We soon learnt they climb cliff walls with far more ease than the Cliff Rescue team we are here to train.

Our bags tossed into our rooms, we reconnoiter the island for likely cliffs to throw rescue bodies off for the night and day activities. It's not hard to find cliffs here – but we need to check the height of each cliff and its stability – most of the island drops steeply to the sea with few places to safely land a boat. One safe place is Flying Fish Cove.

Skirting Flying Fish Cove, we pass the Malay kampong on our way to the Governor's Mansion above the bay, reached by a narrow wiggly road that juts out on steel girders from the cliff-face. The cliff face is garbed in heavy wire mesh which attempts to hold back rock-falls that would easily push a car over the edge. We drive fast, noting even the crabs don't come here much, rather climbing the cliff-face to the plateau than taking the road. Our first cliff accepted, we head for Poon Saan.

The island is populated mainly by Chinese and Malays, with a few Europeans. Most of the inhabitants work at the Phosphate Mine or for National Parks and Gardens. The Malays live mainly in the Kampong on the coast, and daily the sound of their midday prayers and music echoes across the cliff-tops, a pleasant sound at first, becoming annoying as the hour drifts on. The Chinese live at Poon Saan or higher up the mountain, each nationality choosing to live in separation since settlement began. Most Europeans live at The Settlement north of Flying Fish Cove, their simple houses looking out to a blue horizon that seamlessly fuses sea and sky. The sea is calm and sleepy now though some damaged buildings lay skeletal from a cyclone that ripped across the coast years ago. Whether kept as a reminder of the weather's fury or just not yet repaired is hard to tell, for time on the island moves slow.

We soon find out how slow. We need food, but shops on the island don't open till 9 am. They close again mid-afternoon. Wanting to buy lunch, we must wait until 4 pm when their doors open again. Then we can eat until midnight.

The Rumah Tingii Tavern has the best steaks on the island (maybe the only steaks as they fly meat in on Fridays). We dine there many times, walking back each night along quiet roads that skirt the cliffs, accompanied by the gentle kitcher-kitcher-kitcher of red crabs scurrying into the darkness. We encounter our first Robber crab — also known as Coconut crab for its skill of carrying fallen coconuts back up the tree and dropping them; they then feed off the contents through the broken shell. We warn ourselves to stay away from coconut trees. When one giant beast wandered out of the bushes looking more like a turtle than a crab my counterparts moved to the other side of the road, not wanting to incite its nastiness. Unlike our friendly red crabs, this crab attacks and can sever your Achilles with its hydraulic-like claws — claws big enough to feed a small family.

They, like the red crab, are protected, so we quietly sidle by.

On our first day up on the cliff face, our students prepare us for our days of exploring. "Watch out for Pandanus," they say, "also known as Walking Tree. Brush leaf this way, okay. Brush that way, tear big holes in skin." We avoid the giant Pandanus. "Watch out for Maruta Vine," they say, "… called Stinging Bush. Thorns give you rash, make you itch. More you scratch, more you itch." I begin to wonder if going into the jungle is such a good idea.

We go nevertheless as soon as our trainee friends are happily qualified in Rescue from Heights, and I am happily spared from being thrown over any more cliffs.

We become proficient in weaving our way up and down the mountain road, dodging crabs and rusted cars, at swinging round at the ring road that cuts the mountain road onto the coast road. It is now time to go exploring. But the sign at the ring road states all roads, bar one, are closed due to the crab migration, meaning most of the island is now inaccessible.

We drive up to the massive, disused Casino, which is showing signs of decay, the metal on many buildings corroding from the constant sea spray that lashes up the cliff face, laying salt over everything. We visit temples and cemeteries, lookout towers and beaches, Dolly Beach the most memorable. After walking five kilometres along higgledy-piggledy boardwalks through the jungle, the structures built to protect the red crab burrows, and hearing crashing of waves bashing the coastline for much of that time, we eventually stand on a cliff top looking down on a glorious beach, its pristine sands unmarked. Coconut palms sway in the late afternoon breeze as they wait for the sea to wash their feet. Feeling like Tom

Hanks must have felt in *The Castaway*, I capture a hundred photos before the tide urges us back up the concrete stairs to the cliff.

We stroll back through the humid jungle, appreciate enormous Birds Nest ferns in tree tops, edge past serrated Pandanus, gush at porcelain blue crabs and awe the life in the jungle.

We visit The Grotto, a cave flooded by sea-water whenever a wave crashes on the coastal cliffs, the current surging into the cave then receding back. In the afternoon heat and humidity we are tempted to swim, but the rope to be held for safety looks rotted and the old adage comes to our mind: Who rescues the rescuer when the rescuer needs rescuing. Not wanting to be sucked out through the back of the cave and having our trainee friends pull us out of the sea, we move on.

From the lookout on the western cliffs we watch prehistoric-like Golden Bosun, birds found only on this island; they drift on thermal currents escorted by Frigate birds, until they settle on their nests on cliff tops.

That night we taste Robber Crab, poached from the National Park by our miscreant friends. It's a delicacy of grand proportions, obviously the reason they are protected. We dispose of the shells furtively, not wanting to run foul of Federal Police who have jurisdiction over the island.

On our last day we visit the Japanese Cemetery on Phosphorous Hill where headstones have been reverently restored, the jungle cut back so each fallen soul can receive visitors. The ethereal atmosphere is added to by the stifling heat and surrounding crush of Pandanas that rise like church walls, sunlight pouring through the cramped tree canopy like rays through a stained glass window. I feel the movement of souls still walking here.

Our last meal we gather with our friends at a restaurant in Poon Saan and sample every Chinese dish, a sumptuous but low cost banquet.

Our time up, we pack for the midday flight, pray for clear skies, and sadly bid the island farewell. The last few days I have missed patting a dog – only two live on the island – and the sound of country music – of that there was none. We wave the red crabs goodbye, board the plane and soar off the cliff ledge into thick white clouds, leaving our Island Paradise rising from a sleeping ocean until our blissful return.

Just a Doll and a Story

It was just a little Kewpie doll, skirted in mauve netted-lace, spangled with a silvery-purple glitter, its hair painted golden like the tall hooked stick it came on. It hung from that hook on a rod at the back of the carnival stand; had hung there for days, maybe years the way the old man's luck had been running. Nobody wanted to try their luck at his stall these days, he mused as the crowd passed by on their way to more modern amusements. Nobody wanted to toss the ring and loop themselves a prize ... or maybe the game was just too simple to pose a valid challenge any more. But still he smiled and hollered above the bedlam the side-shows created:

"Try your luck; three throws for a dollar. Everybody wins."

But the walkers didn't listen, just kept their eyes to the front and kept going. If business didn't pick up soon, Old Jobe Garrick wouldn't have one, he noted, acknowledging his life was dwindling away into nothingness – had been going steadily that way since Pearl died. And if Old Jobe was down on his luck now, it had started from that sad day. In a few more tomorrows, he would close his tent and wander, for he was barely making enough now to scrape together a meal, let alone make a sustainable living. He just wasn't cut out to be a Carnie anymore. Maybe he never had been, for this was Pearl's life – she'd had the gift to woo the crowds their way; had the smile that drew them to the stand and held them there. She was a mighty special woman, and everyone loved her. Hell, he'd loved her. Still did.

"Try your luck! Three throws for a dollar."

Yep, his luck had gone to the grave with Pearl all right. She'd been the light for both of them, and now he was just a withered old shell with no reason for battling on. He looked up and surveyed the stand critically. It was a lonely place without that woman. He spied the doll, felt a pang of remorse touch his heart with the memory. Above all the little pieces – the fluffy dogs, the china cats, the goofy bears – Pearl loved the Kewpie dolls best; would spend hours at night spangling their plastic bodies, tidying their netted skirts, organising their order on the rack so their colours harmonised. The stand had looked grand then. It was dismal now; dismal, dreary and lonely.

"Try your luck."

Damn bloody luck, he hissed to himself. Without Pearl he couldn't raise enough to replenish the stocks to keep the stand half as good as she'd had it. Hell, he was down to his last of everything: his last meal, his last carnival, his last cigarette, even his last damn Kewpie doll. He had no money to buy any more anything.

For a moment he considered closing the stand right then; take the rest of the day to go and visit Pearl. He spent a lot of time in the cemetery when he came to this town. She'd like this town; said it was bright and held a hope she could feel. Hell, he couldn't feel any damn hope for nothin' no more.

"Try your..."

"Look Daddy, look!" a little girl's voice touched the air, her finger pointing at the old man's red striped stall. "Look, he looks like Grandpa! Oh, and look, there's a doll, Daddy. It's the purple one. I haven't got the purple one."

Old Jobe peered through the passing crowd as it parted like a sea, allowing a tall man to make his way through. In front of him he pushed a wheelchair, in it a child of early age. Jobe assessed her to be about six, maybe seven.

"Please Daddy, may I try? I do so want that doll."

"Try your luck! Three throws for a dollar. Everybody wins." The old man smiled with hope.

The tall man looked weary, rubbed a hand tiredly across his face then pushed it deep into his pocket. "Well, okay…" he heaved a deep sigh, "but this is the last one, Poppet, the last dollar I have on me, so you'd better make it good."

"Oh I will, Daddy. I must. I must have that doll."

"She collects them," he told the old man with a smile, excusing her brash enthusiasm.

Jobe handed the child three rings as the man lined her up to his counter. He took the dollar and dropped it into his own pocket, wondering what was more important to buy, the cigarettes or something to fill his nagging stomach. Strange, right now he didn't much care for Life just wasn't going to get any better.

"She have an accident?" Jobe asked, studying the wheelchair.

"No, she has a bone disease," her father said softly. "Doctors don't like our chances, but we have faith. We must keep hoping."

The little girl looked up, her big blue eyes like china pools in her sweet young face. "You look like my Grandpa," she said brightly, "but he died last month."

The old man smiled down to her. "We all got to go sometime, sweetheart. All got to go sometime."

"I love your doll," she said with a determined smile, "but she looks so lonely."

"Then you'd better throw your rings and get all three to hang on the hooks over there," Old Jobe prompted her gently. It was an easy game and he had no doubt she'd succeed. In readiness he lifted the Kewpie doll down from its rod.

The little girl tossed the first ring, her eyes beaming as it hovered then fell over the highest hook on the board. "I did it, Daddy! I got one."

The man smiled at Jobe. "She's determined. That's why I know she's going to make it."

The second quoit was on its way; it clicked against the backboard and fell over a hook in the middlemost row. Blue eyes sparkled at her achievement. Her father smiled wider. "Now slow down and take your time, Chicken," he warned.

"I have the doll. I know I have the doll." Her hope exuded from her as she flicked the last loop across the distance. It seemed to take forever to reach the back of the stand, seemed to hover indefinitely in mid air before teetering above the bottom-most row, her throw barely reaching the board. Then it tipped the hook, swirled around a few wobbly revolutions then fell to the shelf below with a dull deafening thud. The hook lay empty.

Old Jobe looked at the girl with sympathy, her forlorn face almost shining with tears. Her father shrugged with empathy. "Well you tried, sweetheart. You can't win all the time."

He nodded a thank you to the old man, and eased the chair back into the crowd, the little girl's eyes misting over. "I did try, Daddy... and I did so want that doll. She's so beautiful."

"Never mind," the man said, his voice mingling then fading in the surrounding din.

The ever wandering masses quickly swallowed them up, and they were soon gone from sight, leaving Jobe standing there looking at the doll in his hands. How Pearl had loved those dolls too! he sighed dismally, his loneliness returning.

The tide of heads flowed further down the laneways, their routes diverging and digressing down different paths. How she loved this town, he reflected again. There was hope in this town. Well, he didn't think so, but hell that little girl had hoped.

In a burst of compulsion, he swung his crooked legs over the counter, his wrinkled hand releasing the cord that dropped the red striped awning across the opening. For the first time in a long while, he joined the crush of merry-makers and was carried along in their wake, going where he didn't know but hopeful of finding that unfortunate child. He tucked the Kewpie doll tight in to his chest to avoid it being damaged.

Coming to a fork in the path, well distant from his tent now, Jobe was jostled heavily, the foot traffic deviating in a chaotic mingle as walkers battled to take their chosen line. Amid the battering he lost all hope of finding the little girl and her father, was now just concerned with getting back to the safety of his stand and closing it for good. Struggling to exit the throng, he found a clear patch of ground ahead and pushed his way forward; came to stand on a strip of grass at the fork's centre. From there he turned to survey his whereabouts.

A few feet from where he stood, pulled well back from the hard shoving flow was the man, the child and the wheelchair. Nodding his gladness, Jobe wobbled forward, his old hands holding out the Kewpie doll in front of him.

"Here, please take it," he said to the child. "I'm sure she would be far happier with your other dolls than hanging in my tent alone." The girl's eyes beamed widely, her smile sending a glow of radiance across her pretty face.

"Oh Daddy! Look!" She looked up and behind her to her father, "I told you he was like Grandpa!"

Jobe only smiled, but the expression on the man's face brought it to a quick demise.

"No, we really couldn't," he said, reaching out to stop his daughter's hand from grasping the doll.

"Please, I want her to have it! She tried so hard, had so much hope ..."

The man looked unsure, his hand gone to his pocket, groping, delving into its depths. "I would really rather pay for it," he said, "but honestly, she has played me completely dry."

"I want no money," Jobe said firmly. "I do this because my wife would do this."

The man looked thoughtful. "Please ... I have nothing with me to reciprocate but would you honour us by joining us for dinner?"

Jobe looked surprised. "You don't have to ..."

"Please, Grandpa. Please come." The little girl took his hand in hers, her other clutched the doll safely to her.

"Oh, so it's Grandpa, is it?" Jobe smiled up at the man, then looked down to the child. "And what am I to call you, may I ask?"

"Pearl," she said pertly.

An old man sat rocking on the verandah swing, its rhythmic squeak lulling him slowly to sleep. A child of ten sat on the steps across from him, a box of dolls beside her on the porch. Standing, she walked across and sat on the swing beside him.

"You gave me this one, Grandpa. Do you remember?"

His grey eyes misted as time took him back. "Yes, Pearl. I do remember," he answered wryly. "It's just a little Kewpie doll, but my, it tells a wonderful story."

↝

Kimberley Dream

To wake in my swag with a wide stretching yawn
and be gently caressed by a Kimberley dawn
in a camp that I pitched by a cold rippled stream
is only a part of my Kimberley dream.

White birds overhead that are bickering anew
wing far far away in the Kimberley blue,
to where cockatoos rest in Albizia trees
take my memories soaring on the Kimberley breeze
of crouched round a fire in a mustering camp
huddling to keep warm in the Kimberley damp;
of lying flat out on a pool crystal deep
soothing the skin in the Kimberley heat.
of droving the cattle across the vast plain
or cleansing the skin in the Kimberley rain
or when stepping to ground from a horse that I trust
to sink my feet deep in the Kimberley dust.

When I left this land long time my heart sorely hurt
till I lay my swag back in the Kimberley dirt
In the Kimberley sun or the Kimberley flood
the life in this land is my Kimberley blood.
And now in my swag watching black clouds form
I know it's the first of the Kimberley storms

The changes are coming, no seasonal regret
It's time for the winter - the Kimberley wet
When rainfall eradicates land's steamy haze
giving relief from hot Kimberley days
where far and wide such magnificence seen
rolls on and on in new Kimberley green.

After droving long years in this glorious land
I'll give my bones up to the Kimberley sand
To die in the top-end's a sure-fired must
so my soul can drift on in the Kimberley dust

And now that I've lived to life's journey's end
I let my soul fly on the Kimberley wind
I lie on my swag as life passes me by
'neath a boab tree 'neath a star-filled Kimberley sky

&

Listen

They sing their songs in sonic scales
to tell their tales in dismal wails,
of oceans wide, extinction feared,
of stalwart ships, of men revered.

No tune doth sound of happy creeds,
the singers are a fading breed.
I heed your songs,
You haven't failed.

Sonic soul songs of the Whales.

Moments

You stand on the edge of the wide concrete balustrade, your toes nipping at space as you stare at the blackness below. The water is down there somewhere, way down, swirling murky and brown around the massive concrete pylons before it sweeps away to the sea miles away. You know all that because you stood here yesterday, feet on the cracked grey pavement though as you stared down, watching it roil, wondering where else it touched. You calculated you will wash up on the pretty little inlet by the boat sheds across the river and that it wouldn't take too long for you to get there. Once in, the water's rush would finish you quickly, either the current dragging you under or the fall killing you outright. It would be like hitting concrete. You have calculated your path from the height of the bridge, the strength of the flow and the action of the tide around the headland. Therefore you would most likely be found on the shore, or floating nearby. It wouldn't be fair on Claire if you just disappeared out to sea – she'd think you ran out on her – betrayed her – left her holding the baby, rather than meeting with this ... accident.

All you have to do is sneak your toes out further, wriggle them in your shoes, shuffle, shuffle, till you feel nothing beneath the balls of your feet, as you do now ... then tip a little forward. Would it feel like flying? Would the agony of hitting the water flat on be horrendous? Too late to think about that now ... What would it matter!

You glance along the bridge. That old homeless bum you just emptied your pocket to is scuffing along the walk, shambling along in his baggy grey pants and oversized coat, the smell of old ale and urine strong on the air around him. You grimace that he followed you onto the bridge, a witness that will see Claire get nothing from your efforts. And you don't have time for this!

The old man stops at the railing, glances you up and down.

"I don't have any more money," you say. "I gave you my last dime."

"Just come to say thanks," he says, folding his arms on the railing. Seems like he's settling in to stay. "Mighty generous of you, sonny."

Mighty generous, be buggered, you think. It's just that you have no need of loose change anymore. You will have no need of anything from this moment on. You half smile, not wanting to engage in conversation, and stare blankly down at him.

"You know, I wasn't always like this," the man says, maybe a little embarrassed. "I was real successful once - had a great job, got paid better than most – had big companies trying to woo me over to their payroll. Drove one of those big, flash, black Mercedes and parked it up in my garage. Yeah, I've have my moments. And didn't I shine."

You think: Yeah, I've had my moments too. Life was good when I was shining gold. But shine doesn't stay. It's like, one minute you stand in the sunlight, the next the dark clouds come and tarnishes everything. Only you weren't ready for the storm – you didn't see it coming and got stuck in the deluge without a frigging umbrella.

Understanding a little of what the old man feels, you lean back from the edge.

"Yep. Had a real nice house too," the old man nods. "...a two storey affair up in Glenford Heights, with a great big yard where the kids hung out all day in the pool; the wife there waiting for me every night when I came home for dinner."

Yeah, you think, your toes sliding back from the airiness of space. You know what that was like. Sefton Park, a gated community only the rich and famous could afford. A five by three split level bungalow with three car garage, and an indoor pool and gym. You heave a sigh. Not anymore though. Not anymore.

You stare at the blackness below; glance at the old man again. Is this where you're heading if you don't do this? Is this where this spiralling decline will lead?

"How many kids?" you ask, wondering why he is here on the street. Why is he not with his family?

"Two girls and a boy."

You think that even if the girls don't take him in, he would have a special relationship with his son. He must have done something pretty bad to not be with his son.

"*Had* a son," the old man corrected. "Lost him in Iraq. One of those roadside bombs."

You both remain silent, imagining the mayhem, the loss, imagining the news being delivered home. "That was the start of the end of me and the wife," the old man says. "I supported him joining the Army, she didn't. Didn't take long after our loss for her to finish it for good."

You sigh at his news. At least your lot wasn't that bad. No way would Joel join the Army or Navy. If it wasn't an all out slaughter on the computer screen, he wasn't interested. Maybe that's where you should have put your foot down, you think. Maybe if you'd pushed some issues he'd have grown up with some sense of loyalty to family. Some concern at least. You doubt that he will even notice you've gone, or care. Would any soul care?

"Lost my faith in a bottle," the old man says, looking down to where the mighty river rushes away beneath you. He looks up again, his gaze lingering on your eyes. You wonder if he can see the desperation in them; you wonder if maybe he had stood here once. He gazes back out into the blackness of night, maybe picking up the twinkling of lights over on the headland where you will eventually wash up. Had he maybe also calculated ending it here? It seems he knew what you intended coming up onto the bridge at this bitter cold hour of night. So what do you do now? He obviously isn't going away. If you leave it much longer you won't do it. Just jump, you think. He's too frail to stop you.

"Mmm," he adds. "Lost my faith for a long time. Couldn't see then that things happen for a reason ... everything, son, happens for a reason."

He pulls the collar of his coat higher and you realise you are shivering, that a fine spray constantly wafts past, wetting your hair, dampening your clothes. "Then I realised why I had to go through that ..."

You look down at him. Why does anyone have to go through such pain, such absolute despair? Life is just too hard. You sneak your toes back over the edge of the railing. The wind blustering at your back will make it easy to let go and fly. You can do it, because you simply can't go back to being nothing. You had it all, and in your effort to have more you made stupid mistakes. In your effort to give Claire and Joel everything, to have everything you ever wanted, you took too many risks. And you lost. Lost it all. Oh boy did you lose. You lost the house, the cars. You lost your son's respect. You lost Claire. There was absolutely nothing left ... except your policies. You are at least worth something on those pieces of paper. Claire will realise you did it for her. She could pay off your debts and still be comfortable. You sneak the balls of your feet back out into space. The old man wouldn't tell - he sees your desperation.

The old man sighs. "I needed to realise that all that wealth doesn't make happiness, son. I needed to let that all go to learn what was important in life - that life is about being here for people. Life is nothing without people." He sighs again. "I remember one cold, dark night, I stood about where you are now, wondering why life had let me down, not able to see that things in life steer your purpose."

You stare down into the blackness where the river runs; try to shut out his words. It would be too hard to start again; too hard to win back Claire's respect.

"There was this homeless woman, what we then called a bag lady – she followed me up on this bridge," he says. "Started talking, telling me her sad, lonely story. You know, son, in that moment of giving up I realised I could help her. I could make her life a whole heap better. I realised that helping folk was worth much more than high falutin' houses and fancy cars. I been here helping people ever since. This is my purpose, and losing all that stuff was necessary to bring me here to this bridge." He pulls his coat tighter around him. And you lean out again, loosen your grip on the world.

"And you won't wash up on the cove from here," he says. "The current turns in the middle of the river, and," he skids his palms across each other, "you're straight out to sea."

That will mean Claire won't get a cent, you realise. There won't be anyone to look after her. She will have to pay off all your debts and she'd have a real hard time of that. Your grip locks back on the rail. You pull yourself back in. Sneak your toes back onto solid concrete. A deep heavy weight drops in the pit of your stomach.

"The Lord works in mysterious way, son," the old man says. "And there is always a way out of your problems. You just need people to help you get through it. Why don't you come down from there and we can walk a while; find somewhere out of this cold blessed rain."

Rain? Is it raining? You plop back to the pavement; feel even more a failure that you couldn't even do this right. Nevertheless, it just means better planning next time – like everything else you should have done.

"Come on, son, there's some fire drums over near the alley on the corner. Some nice folk to chat to as well. I can introduce you to Annie. Get you a coat. Light will shine on your day tomorrow," he says as you walk back off the bridge. You can see a gathering of homeless warming their hands perilously close to the dancing flames, an elderly bag lady standing aside watching for the old man's return. You wonder if this was his saviour.

"No, I think I'll go home from here," you say, praying you can sort this out some other way, praying Claire will give you one more chance. You head in the other direction, hands in pockets and bunched against the cold. "Thanks for the chat."

The old man calls after you. "Hey, sonny, you want back your change?" He holds out the fistful of coins.

"Nah! You earned it," you say.

You imagine him, as you walk somewhat defeated, standing around the drums telling all how he'd just stopped a jumper leaping from the East Street Bridge; that he'd just had his greatest moment of all in the sun.

…

Much Ado About Nunning

In the upper hall of Chartreuse monastery, by a stone arch that overlooked the vineyard, Maree-Agnes wriggled her shoulders with irritation. She tipped her head back, tilted it side to side, lifted her chin tightly - anything to relieve the pulling of the wimple as she listened to Antoine tell his plans for the day. Dearly she wanted to prod about inside the dreaded device with a stick to unsnare the wisps of red curls that had caught at the back of her neck; equally she wanted to attack her legs with her fingers for her habit was stiff and scratchy. But she dared do neither. Instead she stayed focused on Antoine.

Dressed in a dark grey robe, his shoulder propped lightly against a tall stone pillar as he spoke, the man gazed down at the rustic landscape that stretched away from the monastery, his mellow voice drifting down the wide stone hall and over the balcony. Maree-Agnes wondered how he tolerated the scratchy dark wool that clung to his smooth gold skin.

She glanced up. Father Sebian had entered the colonnade from the farther end, the priest dressed in a much darker robe than Antoine's. He strode towards them, momentarily observing the same peaceful setting Antoine enjoyed. The rosary beads at his waist clunked and chattered on gold spun cord as he walked, hands palm-over-back clasped in front of him.

"That would have to be Father Sebian," Antoine whispered without looking. "He fairly rattles along."

Maree-Agnes grinned, her cheekbones lifting as her green eyes lit to the comment, the movement pushing her face harder against the wimple, reminding her it was there. Quickly she retracted her mirth. Nuns weren't supposed to laugh. This was further impressed by the old priest's glare as he passed them — the look she had suffered many times in the last few days as she jogged down the corridor, or scuttled up the stairs, her habit cleanly hoisted to clear her booted feet.

She glanced at Antoine when the priest had passed. His lips and chin tight, retracting his own mirth, he remained nonchalant, and continued watching the land beyond the sacred walls.

When Father Sebian had gone, two white-robed novices entered from the other end. They eyed Maree-Agnes and Antoine, tittered behind their hands and hurried on. Antoine shook his head.

"Well Sister Agnes, I had better go and check the gardens," he said, almost with a sigh. Fraternising was not exactly accepted in the nunnery.

Maree-Agnes savoured a last look of his dark wavy hair and close-cut beard. He cut a dashing figure in a frock, she thought as he turned. "And I had better go and check on Phillipe," she considered, it having been a while since she had seen the boy. "He should have finished sleeping by now."

Nodding his approval, Antoine headed to the gardens that spread between the abbey and the road. Maree-Agnes turned in the opposite direction and followed the verandah around the upper floor to the courtyard stairway. From the top of the stairway, she counted five doors down.

The door to her cell stood open.

Instantly she turned cold and scanned the length of the hallway. Rushing forward, she poked her head in through the open doorway. No sign of Phillipe. She leant way out over the white stone railing and scanned the courtyard below. Still no sign of Phillipe. Her gaze swept down across the fountain, forced its way through the immense fronded garden, peered into the shadows of the colonnade beyond.

And she sighed as Phillipe appeared at the far side of the fountain, rippling his hand through the water as he walked around the pond. The boy, small for eight years, was thin, a veritable scarecrow compared to American boys his age; the thought staunched her resolve to serve him well during his stay. If she let down her guard for a second his health could deteriorate rapidly.

Descending to the garden, she made her way to the boy. "Are you all right, Phillipe?" she asked.

The boy nodded.

"You seem to have found your way around all right." She had taken an hour immediately on his arrival from Paris to show him the monastery; made sure he knew where to go for peace, for food, for shelter.

Looking up, the young Israeli nodded. "Yes, Sister. I know my way to the kitchen, to the church, and to our room."

They were to share the accommodation during his stay. "And I know where to find the stairs to the belltower." He pointed to the flight of stairs behind her.

Maree-Agnes refrained from smiling: it was good enough that he knew. But she felt guilty for not smiling, that single lack of response reminding her she lacked the slightest shred of maternal instinct, and she wondered, not for the first time, why this task was hers.

"You may return to the kitchen if you want a snack. You must be hungry by now," she realised.

"Yes, Sister."

As the boy walked away she tilted her head side to side again to free the wisps of hair pulling at her neck, and let her fingers have an inconspicuous dig through the layers of her skirts. At times she considered discarding this woeful habit, but she knew Father Sebian would castigate her with his eyes, and shake his head, and accuse: 'You're a pitiful example of the Order of Dominica.'

Still in discomfort, she watched Phillipe amble along the corridor, her expression tightening when Sisters Beatrice and Margaret stopped to bid him good morning. She did not like the nuns befriending the boy for he was not their responsibility — he was hers and Antoine's. Hers especially. *She* had been tasked to care for him. To educate him as best she could. And above all else, to keep him safe, and that she would do.

As Phillipe moved further down the corridor, she felt niggled that he was gaining distance from her. She knew she should stay closer to him. 'But the monastery is eighty miles from Paris,' her head countered her instincts. 'It is safe and secluded, which is why he was brought here.' Yet intuition prodded her again to stay close.

Phillipe reached the kitchen and entered, and by the time she had caught him up Sister Lumen was feeding him bread. 'Don't be so stupid!' she rebuked herself again. 'He's safe inside church walls! Twenty nuns constantly drift around him. And God protects the innocent. Doesn't he?'

'He's never helped you!'

She said a few *Hail Mary*s for her thoughts and grimaced as she glimpsed Father Sebian strolling across the yard. His disdainful glance told her he considered others more apt to educate this boy. his opinion made obvious at the start of this assignment. But she ignored his thoughts. He did not know.

As the priest climbed the stairs on his way back to his office, Antoine came across the courtyard. "Were you expecting the guardians back today?" he asked with a frown.

She shook her head. "The boy is in care and is to remain so unhindered."

Maree-Agnes went cold again. Father Sebian was not expecting guests, and seldom, if ever, did strangers drop in so far from the city. She leant into the kitchen. "Phillipe, go to the room."

Looking up, the boy's eyes widened, the bread in his hand fell to the floor. "Yes, Sister."

He scuttled out through the back of the kitchen; thin brown legs scampered up the stairs to the upper level where, five doors along, he reached their room. Entering, he slammed the door behind him.

When it shut Maree-Agnes briefly scanned the courtyard. If cars indeed swept along the road, how close were they?

She hoisted her habit knee-high, turned and scurried up the garden stairs to the topmost level. From the tower she could see the spread of land in all directions, a beautiful sprawl of farms and rich green vineyards, where few roads severed the scene. Only one road led to the abbey. On it, two cars were less than a mile away, travelling bumper to bumper.

It was twelve minutes to mass, and Maree-Agnes sighed. Much closer than that and the warning might be misconstrued.

She rang the bell three times. Long peals. The Sisters below scurried, gaggling like geese. That done, Maree-Agnes scuttled back downstairs, her boot heel catching in the hem of her skirt before she reached the bottom, almost toppling her down the last three steps. She almost turned her ankle.

"Shit!" she muttered. Worse, her shoulder smashed against the edge of rough hewn stonewall as she veered round its corner. "Double shit! ... Hail Mary. Hail Mary."

She broke into a run. Sprinting down the wide stone verandah, her skirts hoicked up like a can-can dancer's, she passed three Sisters coming from the chapel. "Hurry, Sisters, take cover," she spurred them on.

They hurried, looking serene and reverent, as if believing whatever happened now was God's will. Maree-Agnes shook her head, yet deep down she wished she could find her faith. She reefed the crisp black habit higher, draped its arduous bulk over her arm and hurried on; dropped back to a walk as she reached the chapel door.

'Far out!' she hissed beneath her breath, 'they could have given a bit more warning than this.'

Six car doors clunked concurrently in the courtyard as she passed through the vestry. She dropped her skirts, adjusted her guimpe and wimple to sit just so, and sedately entered the minster. Serenely, she faced the altar and knelt.

A second later, the large church doors burst open. She counted to ten, her hands pressed firmly together as she stared up at the statue of Jesus. She remained until footsteps entered the church then she rose, turned, and moved down the aisle towards the chapel doors. Outside, the cars were parked one behind the other - she could see them through the open doorway. Six doors meant six men. She wondered, 'Where's Antoine?'

Four black suited men stood across the back of the chapel, each unmistakably Arabic. She scanned their faces, registered minor details as her fingers clutched the rosary at her leg: Al-Mani was one of them.

"Good morning, Sister," the third man from left greeted with a nod. He smiled like a coyote.

"Good morning," she replied with an equally cordial nod. She blinked with soft innocence.

"We are looking for a small boy ..."

Her smile remained friendly, the action pushing the wimple tight against her face, yet this time she forced it to remain so. She kept her eyes from Al-Mani, for the man perused her more closely than she liked. "This is a convent, sir. Why would you seek a small boy here?" The evasion saved her a lie in church, and another dozen Hail Marys. "This is the Holy Order of the Sisters of Dominica."

"So I am told. So you won't mind if we look around then?"

Maree-Agnes went to object but two more men entered the church. One had Antoine's throat firmly pressed by an arm lock, had his arm wrenched up behind him. The second man waved a blue steel Berretta near Antoine's ear, near where blood seeped down Antoine's face.

'They would hit a priest?' Maree-Agnes steamed, but she already expected that. These men were capable of anything, including killing a boy.

"Do you question the word of the cloth?" She hoped to stall them, to give Phillipe more time. But it went unanswered as three men moved down the aisle towards her.

"We simply want the boy," the man reiterated as Antoine, still contained, was shunted towards her. He groaned at the pain inflicted in his shoulders.

Hoping all Sisters had safely taken cover, Maree-Agnes glanced up at the altar, and hoped more strongly that Phillipe would remain concealed within the room that had been prepared for him. Three days they had worked to have it ready so he would be safely contained, and he had been carefully briefed in how to use it. If the worst happened and he was near discovery, he was to scamper through the trap door and sneak up to the bell tower.

"But there is no boy," she lied openly. Anything to save Phillipe. Her eyes caught Antoine's for a mere second; they told her they were in trouble.

Nevertheless, she held her ground, undecided and dallying. She could let the men leave the minster through the vestry and commence their search, taking Antoine hostage with them — which would leave her clear to creep along the rear halls and whisk Phillipe away. She could shepherd him out of the convent and safely away without being detected. Or she could follow Antoine, plead for mercy, and hope Phillipe would stay hidden in his box. She hoped the nuns would abide by the plans they made, and decided she could serve better purpose by saving the life that was now the most in danger. Phillipe, for the moment, was a secondary risk.

To make it harder for the man to pass Maree-Agnes stayed rooted to the aisle, but the man sidled round her and headed for the vestry. Her narrowing of the aisle, however, secured Antoine's release, and he was now only held at gunpoint. Within moments the black suits had exited the vestry and had entered the courtyard beyond.

Maree-Agnes followed behind, her stomach churning that she had one brief chance to save them all – and she mustn't make a mistake. She reached the sunlit garden where the fountain excited water into the pond, where it spurted it up and lobbed it down with a splash; where large fronded palms in large ochre pots waved airily in the breeze. Skirting round the fountain, she scanned the upper verandah. As yet it was empty. Two men, however, had headed for the stairs, one at each end of the lower level. Each had a long nosed pistol drawn.

On the lower verandah two more men opened and closed doors to the Sister's cells, checking each room for Phillipe. She couldn't let them find him.

She scanned the yard and halls for the fifth man, momentarily ignoring the one who still guarded Antoine, the pistol still at his temple. Antoine stared straight at her then glanced at her thigh. She refrained from nodding, noting that his captor's deep brown eyes fixed firmly on her. Two men reached the upper floor and started opening doors. It was now too close.

She stepped forward. "Please don't hurt Father Antoine. Please … please … don't hurt anyone."

She bumped into a palm pot, its sharp corner raking her shin. Reeling with the pain, she moaned and thrust her foot up onto the plant stand, clamped her hand over the throbbing wound then, rubbing vigorously at her leg, she caught up the hem of her habit, hoisted it high and untethered the Uzi from its hiding strap. Within seconds the safety was flicked off and she swung it round and strafed the lower verandah. Two Turks bellowed, smashed against the stonework and collapsed to the tiled floor. Sidling with as much grace and speed as the habit would allow, she cleared the curve of the fountain, gained better view. She spattered another burst along the upper walls. Two more men, pistols raised as they peered down at the sounds below, rent screams upon the air. They rebounded off the back wall, toppled over the balustrade and hit the concrete path with a hollow thud before her.

Maree-Agnes turned the Uzi on Antoine and the man that held him. All was now silent. The Sisters safely shielded in their haven. Phillipe carefully curled up in his box. She swept a glance for Al-Mani, but failed to find him, and knew she'd better look for instant cover. He would fire from seclusion.

Dropping her skirts, she retreated to the nearest stone walkway, and backed behind a wide stone pillar. As long as she was shielded from stray bullets, she could deal with Antoine first, rectify the turn of events that had disadvantaged them.

"It is obvious," the Muslim said, using Antoine as a shield, "we are at a stalemate. I will trade you ... him for the boy."

She shook her head. "I don't trade with terrorists."

"Come now, surely the boy means less to you than the man."

Maree-Agnes stiffened, wondered if her feelings for Antoine were so apparent, for why else would he make that statement? And if that was so, had Antoine detected them? She did indeed love the man dearly. But Phillipe was also important. And a boy. A boy that could ransomly alter a cause she would rather see ended. If Phillipe was found, they would use him as leverage to free Ben Shi-Absolim. And she had not worked the last five years to catch that man to see him ever free again.

"Take him out, Maree, you can do it."

It was true. Antoine didn't have to tell her that. Once assigned, the job was everything. She now had two short choices: pop a shot over Antoine's shoulder and hit the Turk dead centre – with the risk of hitting Antoine if he moved - but if she missed, she might not get another chance before Antoine wore a bullet ...

Movement on the upper floor snatched her thoughts as the fifth door on the upper hall opened, the eternal stillness in the courtyard implying the worst was over. Phillipe stood looking down at her. She dared not give him indication to hide again lest she reveal his presence; she kept her eyes to the Turk.

Her second choice now bore in for two lives hung in the balance. She could punch a hole straight through Antoine, penetrate the Turk at that close range. One shot and she could not miss removing him. The thought made her ill, but she could not allow the slightest chance of Absolim being freed. If Fuerreri, Phillipe's father, had a choice — a choice between saving his son and freeing the world's coldest, bloodiest killer — he would choose his son every time. She knew it. And the peace talks would be damned by his decision.

Steadying the Uzi, she wished she could wipe away the sweat from her hands to secure a better grip.

"Give me the boy," the Turk demanded.

"There is only one thing I'll give you," she said as she raised the Uzi higher. The position drew a better line on the terrorist's forehead.

"If that is your choice then let the priest join me."

Maree's eyes flashed open and 'No!' leapt to her throat. As Antoine's elbow thrust back into the man's mid-section, a short, muffled *pumph* stopped him short of victory. Blood sprayed out towards Maree and a second later Antoine hunched over, grimaced, and toppled forward. Then a second *pomp* sounded sickeningly close to her.

Going cold, she fired her own shot and sent the man levitating backwards. He landed sprawled across the grass, face up, a black hole embellishing his ebony brow like an embedded onyx Indian jewel.

She ducked for cover as a bullet whizzed past her, whistling as it skimmed through her hair. It lodged with a crack in the door frame behind her. She glanced up; saw movement on the upper floor. "Run, Phillipe!" she bellowed as Al-Mani slunk along the wall beside him. He was close. So terribly, terribly close.

The small boy scooted out the doorway and fled toward the belltower — his final sanctuary. Unleashing long red locks as she peeled back the annoying wimple and guimpe, Maree darted forward, one hand still on the Uzi. Stripped to a sleeveless muscle shirt and black habit skirt, she reached the stairs. Desperately she wanted to stop and check on Antoine but Al-Mani was close to the boy — closer than she'd ever dare let him be. She could only hope Phillipe was swift, and that Antoine could hold on till she returned.

Clutching the habit skirt and hoisting it high again, she took the stairs two at a time. Al-Mani was on the higher staircase by the time she reached the first. Of Phillipe, there was no sign. For the first time in a long, long time she prayed; prayed for them both.

At the top of the third flight, she reached the belfry, sidled into the room and, pressing her back against the wall, kept her raised weapon pressed against her breast so it could not be ripped from her. Al-Mani however was on the other side of the platform. Stooped over, he scrutinised the platform and the parapet beyond. But he saw nothing.

Maree aimed her weapon, drew closer to the bell shaft, and glanced briefly down it. The drop was a long way down. She checked her ammo clip. There were too few bullets left for any mistakes.

Al-Mani turned from his search, took momentary store of who she was and smiled, amused. "I see they teach unusual Scripture here," he said. "Or does the CIA insist on you finding your God?"

His words haunted Maree — her answer too close to the truth. "We can't afford religion. We might feel guilty."

He smiled more widely, cunning, his white teeth showing as perfect as a line of polished headstones. Yet his black eyes sparked with intensity.

Maree moved around the platform, the Uzi still high and ready, her finger itching to squeeze off the shot. But she resisted. The thought of finding God prodded her, for what she had done to Antoine.

Al-Mani raised his hand gun. "I guess it is with me as it is with you ... the job is not finished until it is done." He glanced back over the balcony, still looking for Phillipe.

She nodded, her green eyes locked to his. Those black evil orbs would be the only sign that her end was nigh. And there it was. A flash. A sudden glimmer deep within the black. She squeezed the trigger, the force of release lifting the barrel sharply. His pistol barked also and she turned sharply away. A bullet whacked into the upright where she had stood, ripped the timber beside her face and whirled it past her ear. She watched Al-Mani stagger, reel backwards; watched as he hit the solid railing, arms flailing as he tumbled out into no-man's land. He would hit the rooves below with a resounding thud, and move no more. She listened to the crack of breaking roof tiles then sidled to the edge, checking her correct assumption. 'That was for Antoine.'

Her lips pursing at the grim image below, she nodded then shouldered the weapon. There were important things still to do.

Leaning over the deep wooden shaft, she called, "Phillipe, you can come up now."

The small boy shinnied back up the knotted bell rope, foot over foot like a macaque monkey. She gripped his skinny arm and helped him back to the platform. When he looked at her for approval, she smiled. "Okay, you can ring the bell now."

Satisfied with Al-Mani's retirement, she descended the stairs to the garden. Phillipe was safe, but she needed to know something more.

As she reached Antoine, the bell stopped ringing; its echo drifted across the land; over the courtyard. Antoine lay on the ground staring up, blood oozing through his fingers from a hole in his left shoulder. More blood seeped down the grey woollen cloth. She bent over, tears burning behind her eyes as she looked down at him.

His dark eyes blinked. "Is it over?"

She nodded, and smiled.

He started to rise. "I'm sorry I missed it. I bet you did some heavy praying up there."

Maree scratched at the itch on her upper thigh. "I don't know how to pray."

Antoine's eyebrow rose and he scowled as he came to his feet. "Maybe someone should teach you."

Unsheathing a knife from the scabbard strapped to her calf, she deftly slashed a large sward of cloth from the habit's hem and stuffed it under Antoine's hand to stem the bleeding then she scratched the itch again.

"My, your habit is annoying," Antoine smiled, "but I must say you look pretty good in a dress."

"So do you," she said, realising this was the first time he had seen her in one. She rubbed at the tension building at the back of her neck. Compliments from Antoine, few as they were, almost made her blush. Always made her heart zing slightly faster. But, he was married, and the pictures now playing in her mind meant she was a couple of hundred Hail Mary's behind.

❧

Neither Lie, Douglas

Two tousled headed boys were sitting on the curb of their leafy suburban street, one keenly watching the traffic that whizzed by on the busy intersection further up, the other studying a puddle that had been left from the recent rains, taking particular note as a silent plummeting droplet from the overhanging tree above plopped and disturbed its surface. He leant further forward over his knees, catching the other boy's attention.

"What are ya doin', Douglas?" the second boy enquired with a frown.

"Readin' puddles," came the youngster's droll reply.

"How do ya read puddles?" the enquirer smirked again. "Ya can't even read. Ya too young."

"I can read puddles!" Douglas quipped back offendedly, scratching at the freckle line across his nose.

"How?!" came the scoffing remark. "Show me how!"

"It's easy," the little boy said. "You just have to look. Just look into the water and you can see all sorts of things."

The older boy leaned forward sceptically. "Like what?"

Douglas waited for the ripples to clear, waited for the smooth reflection to cast its vision before his eyes then he started reading – the only reading his young age was capable of. "I can see a tree," he said. "It's a street tree, all green an' yellow an' wet. And it's going to be a big tree." A drip-stirred ripple clouded the pool for a second then all was still again.

"I can see a blue sky," the little boy advised next, "an' it's clear so there won't be any more rain today." They were wise words from an only just five year old, and the other boy looked up in verification, sensed there was more to this puddle reading than met the eye, and leant forward closer.

"I can see you," Douglas said, turning his head to look straight at the ten year old, a hint of affection showing.

"Yeah? And what can ya tell about me?"

"The puddle says Andrew will be my friend." He looked up hopefully, yet caught the other boy's face hardening a little.

"Did it now?!" came the teasing retort, but he had caught the despairing plea from the lonely little boy who had just moved in next door.

"Uh huh. The puddle says so ... an' puddles don't lie." He shook his head earnestly.

"How do ya know that?!"

Douglas's face tightened in defence. "My Daddy says so. Puddles don't lie!" His voice was adamant.

"Okay ... okay," the older boy pacified him without commitment. "So what else do you see?" he dodged the subject.

"Sometimes I see Mummy's face in the puddle."

Andrew frowned again. All the things the little boy had seen had actually been there, and he flashed a quick and worried glance behind them to Douglas's house.

"But you can't. I heard she's ..."

"I can!" Douglas protested. "I can see her! Daddy said I can! An' I see her in the puddles ... any time I want!"

Andrew detected immediately the great sense of loss the little boy was feeling. He'd lost his dog in the year just gone and although it wasn't quite the same, he understood that sense of being so alone.

"... an' if it's not raining, I can see her in the clouds," Douglas prattled hurriedly, desperate to convince the other boy.

"Yeah. I know ... She's an angel, isn't she?" Andrew said, remembering how his parents had handled his grief.

"Uh huh. Daddy said so."

Andrew rose to his feet, stepped back from the curb as the school bus rounded the corner to his street. He pulled Douglas up and moved him back a safe distance.

"Well, puddles and Daddys don't lie, Dougie. They don't lie," Andrew smiled as the bus braked beside him. "I'll see you after school, matey."

Douglas smiled back, first at Andrew, then as the bus pulled away and the puddle cleared, at his mother's fading reflection.

&

On 66th Street

For long moments he stared up at the church steeple, its shadow shading his face as the sun sank towards the distant hills. People brushed past him as they went on about their business, but he paid no heed; he was too aware of the darkening pavement, of the sun losing its heat, of the wide stone cross that stood indelibly across his eyes, and the crucifix that felt so hot against his skin. It hung on a chain around his neck, had hung there for as long as he could remember.

"Never take it off, Frankie," his mother had always told him. "Not when you bathe; not when you swim, and never when you sleep! You must never take this off."

He hadn't taken it off, almost never in his entire lifetime. Oh he'd wanted to at times, sometimes badly, compelled by some strange voice that raged in his head, the deep-throated sibilance wanting him to throw it into the grave on top of his mother.

"She's bound you with this chain," the voice had said. "She's trapped you with her insistence. Be free! Be free! Free yourself! Let *her* wear the chain for a change. Throw it, boy! *Throw it ... NOW!* Give her the greatest gift you can, seeing she was so fanatical over it!"

He remembered his hand had gone to the chain, had clutched the cross tightly, and, as the voice hissed on, he'd increased his pressure, the chain biting hard against his flesh, just a shade off breaking. Then his hand had seared, the metal burning into it, branding his skin with a blackened mark he would wear to the end of his days, the agonizing heat making him release his hold.

"Never take it off!!" burned just as viciously across his brain.

He stood now outside the church, knowing he must enter before dark, yet now he was here he was reluctant to do so. Something was holding him back, something stopping him from climbing those few short stone steps into the sanction of the church. Yet he must. For his own safety, he must.

He looked around, confused, for he'd never felt this before. Always since his mother's death he had felt the urgency of being in a holy place before darkness fell, and always he had hurried to the nearest blessed ground as the sun had set. As he had this day. But now ...

Behind him, across the road, shadows faded in the park; people hurried home from their day's toil, hurried to be back with their families, and he wondered if they knew how dangerous the night really was.

On a bench at the edge of the road sat an old, old man, a priest, he noticed by the collar and bib beneath the heavy jacket. He was a smallish man, if he estimated correctly from the way he sat, his arm stretched out along the back of the seat, one leg crossed casually over the other. His white hair ruffled loosely above incredible piercing blue eyes, giving him an aura of immense holiness, wisdom and truth. He stared at him, wondering, for he'd travelled that road before - the road of trust. He was smarter than to ever do it again.

"Good evening, Father," he said politely then turned promptly back to the church. *Trust no-one*, he warned himself. *Trust only in yourself. Now enter the church! Quickly.*

"You look troubled, my son."

The words came from behind him, smooth and mellow, in tones that spoke of assurance, of peace, of follow-the-path-of-righteousness,-my-son. Smooth as smooth. He dared not listen to the tone for it could indeed deceive. Glancing back, he found the man now stood behind him, the blue eyes kind yet assessing him with caution.

"No, Father," he lied, "I am not troubled." Immediately he felt at odds with himself for lying to a priest, and felt irked at having called the man *Father* for he'd never had one of his own, and the word always hit that point savagely home. His hand went to the crucifix which lay beneath his shirt and he added, "I am merely in two minds."

The priest nodded slowly, his eyes still assessing his dark brown eyes, blue-black hair, his mid-twenties stature, the broad, solid structure and dark skin tone of his southern Italian heritage. He looked up. The sun was tipping just below the centre arm of the stone cross at the high point of the spire. "You will be late for Mass if you do not hurry," the priest said.

Frank looked at him with regret. "It is not the Mass I go for, Father," and looked duly surprised that the priest was neither puzzled nor shocked by his words - he simply nodded that he'd heard and looked up at the new oak doors which were open to the street.

"Not everyone does, my son."

Frank liked the way those words sounded. *My son.* It always sounded so solid, gave him a sense of belonging. Yet it wasn't a sense of belonging to the church for he was in no way religious. Not like his mother had been. Oh sure, he'd slept in the room with the shrine of the Madonna above his head. He'd carefully dusted the ornaments of Jesus on the cross and others of the Virgin Mary when he'd helped her with the housework. But he was far from believing; far from being the devout Catholic she had been. *What God would deny a boy his father! What God would make a child suffer wondering who his father was? What God would inflict him with the voices that were slowly driving him crazy?*

Am I already insane?

"I don't even know if I believe," he said openly, surprised that he had admitted it. To this day he had told no-one, not even his Mother. *So what does that make you? A hypocrite? You sleep in churches for Christ's sake! Or are you just trying to shock the priest?*

"Yet you sleep in churches?" the priest asked, one eyebrow hiking to mock him.

Frank spun back to the man, shocked. *He read my mind! Beware of him!* He tried to hide the fear growing inside him. *Go inside. Enter the church, you'll be safe there.* But he did not move, his feet still reluctant to enter the new stone building before him. Instead he said, the words falling out without his intention, "The voices stop when I'm in the church. I can only sleep when the voices stop."

"Why?" The man looked at complete ease with himself as he stood looking at the lowering sun. "Do they bother you?"

"Yes. They frighten me." Frank suddenly realised the priest had not asked *What voices?* and thought: *He knows! My God, he knows!*

"Then you had better enter the church, Frank. You had better hurry for the night is coming fast."

Frank suddenly went cold. "You know who I am?"

"Yes, I had an idea. They said you would come. They said that one day you would come."

"Who said?"

"That is not important. But ..."; he pointed up to the red orb that was now sinking to the height of the pitched church roof. "... you must be aware of the darkness. Should you not go inside?"

Frank felt even colder. He shook his head; felt breathless, as if the whole world was bearing down on him, as if his life was fast coming to an end. *What's wrong here? I feel so doomed, yet the chain is still on.* His hand again felt the cross beneath his shirt. *It must be him. He is pushing me to my end. I can feel it. Get away from him! Quickly.* But instead he said: "I feel I cannot enter the church tonight."

Despaired, he rubbed a hand firmly over his face, that feeling of doom prodding strongly each time he thought of climbing the stairs. He was doomed if he entered, doomed if he stayed. Only the soft voice of the man beside him made him feel safe, yet it was pushing him forward to the church.

He looked across at the man. A wide, delighted smile had spread across the priest's face, his eyes flashing with similar emotion. "Then walk with me, my son. Walk with me, the darkness will wait a while longer."

NO! Go inside!! Go inside! Do it now!!

But the priest had taken hold of his elbow and was gently guiding him away from the church, away towards the crosswalk which led to the park. "You are still wearing the crucifix, no doubt," the man asked. Frank nodded, his mind screaming: *Beware! Things are not as they seem!*

He remembered Rosa, his girlfriend, who had constantly prompted him to remove the chain. "It sticks into me, Frankie," she'd say. "Take it off, Frankie." Or the time she had wanted a token of his love. "Give me the chain, Frankie. I will wear it for you." He had loved Rosa, and he'd allowed her to take the chain from his neck. Immediately he'd felt strange, his body emptying then refilling again, and he felt ugly with its rebirth. He felt mean, and he'd hit his mother, and stolen from his neighbour. Worst of all, he'd enjoyed it. Then Rosa had left him; she had hurled his chain from the window, and had laughed, cackling insanely that *He* had won.

When he had slept, the voices came, compelling him to other deeds, deeds that churned his stomach; that demanded more hurt be inflicted on his mother. He didn't want to obey, but something deep inside him overruled his wishes, and he had. But his mother had been waiting for him, as if knowing he was coming for her, and she'd splashed him with water that burned him fiercely. He'd cried out in pain, and writhed upon the ground, and she had leapt upon him and secured something tight about his neck. The pain he'd felt then was more excruciating than the burning acid-water, his body lurching until sharp, spasmodic jerks exhausted him. Then he'd hit his head, and all had gone dark.

When he'd awoken, all was normal again. He felt normal, the burns on his skin were gone, the crucifix back on his neck. Blissfully, he felt kind again, though the bruises about his mother's face wrenched him deeply, and he'd cried into her shoulder as she caressed him. "Never, Frankie," she had said, "never take off the chain. Promise me."

"I promise, Momma. I'll never take it off again."

She'd refused to tell him what had happened to him when he'd asked her; she'd simply said he'd had a bad, bad dream, but her bruises told him otherwise. Whatever had happened, he knew he never wanted to feel that way again, and he knew he must never trust anyone ever again. Just her. And, when she died a few years later, the victim of a hit and run driver, he knew he could trust no-one. She alone had been his saviour, and the gap she had left in his life had opened the door to the voices.

They now plagued him, coming with the darkness and leaving with the dawn. They taunted him. Teased him. Sent him nearly crazy. One night, almost blind with the incessant hissing sounds, he had burst into a church and yelled, "Save me, God. Save me."

That night, curled up on a pew, feeling no cold, and no fear, hearing only peace all around, he had slept the best sleep of his life. No-one had prompted him for endless hours: Take off the chain. Take off the chain.

He looked back at the priest. "I never take it off," he said candidly.

Again the priest smiled. They were crossing the road to the park.

Go back to the church, Frank. This is a trap. Go back to the church. But he couldn't. He was totally mesmerised by the man, and the voice, and a strange sense of knowing that something was happening. His throat going dry, he had asked, "How do you know who ...?"

"Are you afraid of the dark, Frankie? It is getting late."

Frank looked back to the west. Only a sliver of sun still sat above the church roof. He had a little time. "Not *that* afraid just yet, Father. I still have a little time," he said, yet he was aware that the face of the old stone church on the opposite side of the park was falling into darker shadows, the two holy facades splitting the city into faces of old and new.

"Good, then I shall tell you a story. It is the story of a life-time."

The thought suddenly washed over Frank that this was a stall tactic; that the priest might try to keep him talking till darkness was fully on them, that if he knew about the chain and the crucifix he might try and take them from him. He looked up, warning himself to stay alert to the sunset, warning himself to remain within reach of the church. There were two of them now he noted, and he could reach either within minutes if he ran. He let his eyes drift back to the priest.

"Once there was a good woman … a lady of the church," the priest began. "She was a Nun of the Order of St. Domini in Rome, and she was the most beautiful Nun any of us priests had laid eyes on." The priest looked up at Frank to make sure he was truly listening, aware that the man's thoughts flitted back and forward from him to the sunset. "One day, this Sister, we shall call her Mary Veronica for the story's sake," he said, "was suddenly wrenched from the very church doors, abducted, stolen if you will by assailants unknown. She was a young girl at the time, and no-one saw her for many months thereafter. It seemed she had been plucked from the very face of the earth.

"When she did return to the church many months later she was heavily pregnant and swore upon the altar that she had been overcome at darkness, imprisoned by a band of men in capes and hoods and taken to a place where a ritual was taking place, a ritual where she was mated with the Devil. Few believed her story, as you can imagine," the man went on, thoroughly pleased now that he had the young man's attention, and that the glow of the sun was barely visible over the roof of the new church. The streetlights around and the lights within the park were slowly coming on.

"However, because of her distress and her consistent insistence that her story was true, the church saw to her welfare and tended her until the child was born, her father and mother having abandoned her when they heard of her dilemma.

"Mary Veronica delivered a baby boy in the year of '67, a baby who screamed the church down, a baby who was tortured by pain even though physicians could find no physical problem with him. Because of this, it became necessary to find the child alternative accommodation, *and* for Sister Mary Veronica who refused to give him up, as the church was having difficulty in maintaining its order under those circumstances. Mary begged the church to let her and the child stay as she was convinced the child would die if it left the protection of the church, yet it seemed to be dying anyway.

"Her pleas, however, were to no avail and she had to leave. Only when she had found alternative parents for the child could she return to her Order and resume her duties. As she was shepherded from the church, the child cradled tightly in her arms and still screaming in pain as it had done since its birth, Mary fled from her escorts. She ran across the church yard and into the church where she fell upon the altar ..."

The sun was now dipping halfway below the horizon, and Frank hadn't noticed, nor had he noticed how far they had wandered from the church on 66th Street.

"I was but a young cleric in those days," the priest reminisced, "but I will remember her words till the day I die. She called upon God, crying. She asked him to have mercy on her and the child. She asked him to bless young Francis and protect him with his love and grace for he had asked not of his pain or birth. He was a product of the good in her and of evil, and she asked Him to show him that good could endure. 'Protect him, dear Lord,' she cried, 'or he will die. Punish me, but protect the child.'"

The priest glanced sideways at the young man and read the understanding dawning in his eyes. Yet there was also skepticism, so he played out more of the story. "As I stand here, with my word sworn on the Holy Bible, I will never forget how that crucifix appeared in the air, falling it seemed from the hollow point of the spire within the very church itself. Falling from the highest point, it seemed to drift, tumbling slowly in a golden-yellow haze, on a chain, and I swear I heard the angels sing that day. And I heard the words, 'Mary, you must leave and take the child. Protect him with your life, and with this on him forever protect the world.'

"The cross fell at Mary's feet and she picked it up, and crying, placed it round the baby's neck. That baby, my son, stopped screaming in that instant, and fell asleep in her arms, totally at peace, and out of pain, no longer slowly dying. The Devil, you see, can never walk on holy ground, and nor can those spawned of the Devil. This child was reborn by God's love, though seeded by the Devil's loins, and he was blessed by the Almighty himself. With that, he survived though Mary Veronica bore her punishment and was sent from the church. She came to America where it was felt the baby would be safest, and until her death, she followed God's word and kept the child safe."

The sun was down now and the priest stopped walking and looked at Frank with concern. "Do you understand the story?" he asked.

Frank was unaware of the darkness as he stood beneath the park lights looking down at the man. "I understand the shrines now," he said. "I think I understand many things."

"I have known of your torment since your mother died, Frank," the priest said. "And I know of your torment in not having a father ..."

Frank stood silent. *Do I really have a father? After all these years?* He wiped a hard hand over his face. *Can I really believe any of this?*

No. It's just a diversion! You've been tricked!

Suddenly he became aware of the night.

"I was sent here to help you make your choice, and it is time now, Frank, to make that choice." The priest looked up at him frankly, the blue eyes showing nothing but an understanding that this was indeed the time. There was no excitement, and no regret - just the time. "You are standing on the very border, son, and the darkness is all around you. Choose which path you take."

Anger smeared Frank's face. This man was a Demon. He had held him after dark. "I take only one choice, and that is to go to the church."

"Ah! But which church, Frankie?" the man asked.

Frank looked across the lights above the new church where he had stood an hour ago then across to the old Gothic church with its dimly lit entrance. He knew what the priest had meant for he was standing mid-way between the two. Which one should he run to? Did it matter which one protected him?

"It doesn't matter which church, old man. I told you, I have no religion."

"No. You only have the Lord. But remember, the Devil works with false facades. You must be aware of this before you enter."

Frank frowned. *What does he mean? He's screwing with my head! Get inside a church, Frank, for God's sake!*

The priest stood his ground, one eyebrow raised, waiting for Frank's decision. A short while ago, he was heading for a church, waiting for the darkness so he could enter, the next he was the Devil's son – *at least you have a father now* – and having to decide which path to take. *And what did he mean, false facade? The church has a false facade? Well the man himself could just as easily have a false facade.*

"You're the Devil," he said sharply to the priest, for the man had succumbed him to the night. Soon the voices would have him. Soon they would insist he take off the chain. They would penetrate his mind until he could resist no longer.

"I think there is a little bit of the Devil in all of us," the man said, "but it makes little difference now. You are standing on the threshold, and must decide who to follow. Which Father will you heed? You cannot run forever."

It was all too much for Frank. Both hands pressing against his ears, he tried to rid the story from his mind; tried to fight back the voice's insistence, both from with inside his head and without. He turned quickly and started to run. *None of this has happened!* he steeled determinedly. *None of this is real.*

Go back to the church, Frank. Go inside the church. He ran for 66th Street, the priest's voice calling after him: "Remember, the Devil, Frank. He works in strange ways. Listen for the angels' voices."

He glanced back only once, and saw the man walking calmly away towards the other church, and thought him the Devil's Advocate.

Racing along the pathway, he reached the park gates and bolted out into the street. There were no cars coming so he didn't stop. *Get inside the church, Frankie. Get inside the church.*

He reached the bottom step and started to climb.

False facades. False facades. Listen for the angels' voices. There's a little bit of the Devil in us all.

He reached the huge oak doors, the voices ringing loudly in his head. He looked up, and saw the large number six above his head. *Go inside, Frankie. Six 66th Street. Six 66.* The voices in his head urged him on.

Which Father will you follow? Seeded by one. Given life by the other.

Come inside, Frankie. It's dark out. Come inside. But first take off the chain! Take off the chain!

"NO!" he yelled, the words ripping from his throat. "*NO!*"

Turning, he sprinted away from the false new church, the church which had been built on unhallowed ground. He raced away, back down the street and across to the park. He could see the church across the way clearly through the darkness, as if it was awash with golden haze, its purity rising up to meet him. And he could hear the voices, angels singing gloriously, choiric voices drifting out the doorway and down the street to meet him. That was what had stopped him entering the church on 66th. There were no angels' voices, just insistence.

Breathing deeply, he climbed the stairs to the Lord's safe Haven, slowly, his eyes resting on the priest who stood serenely just inside its open doorway.

"Father, I am not a religious man," he said, yet this time that word sounded so right to use, and he wondered if he was telling untruths.

The man's hand landed gently on his shoulder, guiding him inside. "Aren't you, my son?" he asked placidly. "Aren't you?"

❧

Resolutions

She stood on the edge of the platform looking down its interminable length. In ten minutes the 9.15 train would come hurtling through from Causham. Shortly after that the silver streak of the non-stop run from Epsom to Durridge would fly by whizzing her hair and scarf into a riotous mess.

She strained to see the lights in the distance but the 9.15 train was still too far away and there were numerous bends between Cumbridge and Causham.

She sighed, deeply. Ten minutes and a miniscule second was all that was left of this worn out, decrepit old hag of a woman. Ten minutes and a brief shunt was all that held her from her maker. Nine minutes and thirty seconds.

She edged a little closer to the sudden drop. People further along the station milled about waiting patiently for the 9.20 that would take them to the city to arrive. A group of teenagers ballyhooed each other in mock argument, then laughed.

How grand it must be to be young, she thought whimsically. How grand it would be to have the time to undo all the mistakes one makes in life. Unfortunately, she realised not for the first time, the older she got, the less time there was to rectify the horrid mistakes she made.

Now time was too short. There would be no undoing. She would go to her grave without resolving her errors. The errors she'd made could not be undone.

Glancing down the platform she checked that no-one was aware of her closeness to the wooden rim of the station landing. Her toes were almost nipping over the edge of the wood.

Nine-ten. Five minutes.

She had chosen this exact time to remedy her errors the only way she could, purely because if she felt weak-hearted at the nine-fifteen she had the silver streak close behind it. One slip and it would all be over.

She wondered if Simon would ever find out. She wondered if there would be any great reaction. Then she shook her head. Probably not. How could you love some-one you didn't know? How could you miss them?

She glanced down the platform again. There was a light in the distance. This was it!

As the light grew larger and brighter, she shuffled almost inconspicuously closer to the drop below which sat the insidious steel tracks. Briefly she wondered what she would feel as she was crushed and shattered and severed beneath the iron wheels. But she pushed the thought back. She mustn't think! She mustn't imagine! She must just step out. She must step out at 9.15.

A huge white ball obliterated the distance, and the bends, and the tracks, and the station. All she saw was the hurtling light of the 9.15.

For a second she saw Simon. She saw Simon at the moment of his birth. She saw Simon at the moment he was first lain in her arms. She saw Simon handed back to the nurse for the last time. She saw Simon being placed in his crib and his crib carefully lifted into the back seat of a car. She saw Simon at five years old. How smart he looked in his short pants suit, his hair slicked neatly back and covered with a cap.

She saw Simon as a young man making his way in life. She saw Simon opening his new offices on Rochelle Street, and the smart young lady that now graced his arm. She saw Simon walking tall down the boulevard with reporters chasing after him. How well he handled himself in public. How proud a young man he was.

She saw Simon as she saw him on TV, the congressman, the lawyer. She heard the slander sheet reporters questioning his past, his heritage and heard Simon say how he was endeavouring to find his family. One day soon he would find his family.

The bright white light now filled her vision. One day he would find her.

She saw Simon, his dark wrath of hair ruffling, his white teeth gleaming as he announced he had news that would soon enable him to be reunited with his mother. Oh Simon, she thought desperately. Why couldn't you leave well enough alone?

The white light now filled her mind. Nine fifteen. She stepped out.

Someone shouted.

A dark shadow raced across her as the child was ripped from her mindful arms for the last time.

The newspapers next day reported, "A bag lady, known to all around Rochelle as Give-a-care Annie, slipped tragically to her death from a railway platform last night. Authorities are investigating how the accident occurred. Congressman Simon Dalton said last night that Annie's death could have been avoided had Government approved the funding for the Homeless of Rochelle.

"Annie was a regular face around the streets of our city," he said. "She will be sadly missed."

∾

Riding On Trains

We sat there in the plush leather seats, our bodies swaying in unison with the roll of the long carriage as we peered out the wide glass window.

"Look, there's a meadow with horses in it," Peter cried.

"Oh look at them running," I gushed as the train swept by them. How I loved to see horses running - it was almost as good as riding on trains. One day I was going to be a famous horse-riding person.

"Oh look, there's a tunnel coming up near the bend," Peter cried again.

The train whistle went "Woo, Woo Woo," as the engine disappeared inside the dark cavern, as our bodies rocked and swayed with the rhythm of the carriage.

We closed our eyes, afraid of the darkness, smelt the acrid layer of smoke as it billowed past us.

"Woo, Woo Woo," the train whistle went again as it exited the tunnel. Moments passed.

""You can open your eyes now," Peter said. "We're clear."

I opened my eyes, and sure enough, bright blue skies laced with fluffy white clouds were again outside my window.

"Oh, look. We're going to cross a bridge," Peter cried.

"Oh yes, look at the bubbling river," said I, lifting my feet as the train rattled over, my heart in my mouth that there were no sides to the bridge and what if we fell off the tracks and into the water.

"Did you see the fisherman?" Peter asked.

"No, I didn't," I said, annoyed at being such a scaredy cat.

"Well, he was there," Peter declared.

I didn't doubt it. Peter always saw such wonderful things on our train rides.

"Oh look, there's a circus on the road. Look at all their wagons. And look, elephants. I count six," said Peter.

I shook my head. "No, there's eight. And look at all the ponies. Oh, wonderful, wonderful ponies."

"Woo Woo, Woo," went the train whistle.

"We're coming to a crossing," said Peter.

Our bodies rocked and swayed more violently as the train crossed a roadway and sped on towards our destination.

"Are we going to have lunch on this ride?" I asked becoming hungrier and hungrier the further we travelled.

"Mummy said she was getting us sandwiches," Peter advised. "We just have to sit here and be good, and she might even get us a special treat."

Ooh, a special treat. But my special treat was already happening as fields of green and gold dashed by my window.

"Right, now," said Peter, "it's my turn to be the train driver."

"Oh no it's not!" Claire protested. "We haven't gone nearly far enough yet."

"Oh don't go, Peter," I begged. "I love to see the fields and bridges through your eyes."

I felt him tuck the blanket further in around my sides.

"Oh, … all right," he said. "You just stay nice and warm. We'll head down the hill to the snowfields next and see some polar bears."

I gazed out the cold blank windows that were my eyes, and waited with high expectation.

⊱

Serpent River

Rain trickles down
wets corrugations
dampens red earth
smothers dust.
Black feet patter as the sky darkens
white grins brighten
as children, dressed as punk rockers
squeal and laugh
Dogs shake mangy coats now moist with nature's gift
and a cat slinks under the verandah

Beyond the camp
beneath the pregnant boabs
elders sit
palms outstretched to the wet
old eyes narrowing.
They rise as one from the riverbank
move back to the humpy
gather up belongings
from this belonging place.

The sky now rumbles
as old men gather women
quieten children
move aside the dogs
and take their place heading for the bush.

Soon the serpent spirit will rise
to overtake the river
overtake the land
move them on to new places
move them into new times
Time has spoken of this journey's need.

They will return when the bush returns
when the Serpent spirit births new places further on
when his presence no longer lingers on the land —
when the wet is over.

Study Time

I watched a moth die this morning,
heard it first
then saw it drop from the ceiling to the shelf,
thought then it was a shame,
that its days were numbered.

I looked closer,
saw it breathing still
and felt better.
Maybe it was only resting,
and pondered idly if those delicate
creatures ever really slept in their short life,
then went away to busy myself with
more important things.

I came back some time later
to engross myself in rigid print and study
and was deep within that toil
when he dropped again,
landed, right before my eyes
and there he died,
took his last breath,
his last flutter,
and then was still.

I groaned
and watched him longer,
studied his dirty brown tonings;
thought that he should be an ugly thing,
yet somehow he wasn't.

That dirty brown was sheeny, silken soft,
intricately grained with black and beige,
a graphic pattern climbing and declining
along the feathery scalloped wing
foreshadowed only
by a pair of perfect peacock-tail green eyes.
And he sat there taut before me
propped on his foreclaws
with his wings dipped to caress the ground,
poised as if ready for flight;
like a bomber on the tarmac tensely waiting
to scramble skywards
just begging for the siren to alert it,
or my hand to disturb.
So I did.

I touched it, saying
'Fly and be free, my pretty,'
but it just fell on its face,
nose-dived,
the horizontal feeler prop dipping earthward,
kinking,
its sheeny wings crinkling,
the foreclaws crumpling beneath it.
And I felt sad.

I couldn't bury that moth you know —
it was much too beautiful for that,
so I put it in a matchbox
and sighed it a prayer.
Then I cursed it
for it had ruined my day
my thoughts now gone on who he was
and did he have a family that would miss him.
Poor chap.

No room for study now.
No room for more important lessons
so I left him sleeping in his matchbox
on the desk
and went outside in the sunlight
to ponder humanity
and death.
I watched a moth die this morning.

❧

The Birthday

Enid Bellamy sat in her comfortable chair, in her comfortable room, in her very comfortable house in Wiggam Street. She knitted, for she was waiting, and what better way to while away the time than to lengthen the garment that clung supportively in a hundred or so places along the breadth of the needles. The clock on the cabinet behind her read seven o'clock precisely, the time not overly pressing at her conscience for the family were not due until the half hour.

Looking up, she noted her appearance in the mantel mirror, a glorious long hanger with fluted edges and a smoky image of galleons and oceans in the lower left corner. It was an heirloom and she liked where it was displayed for at any time of the day she could touch up her hair or face, or just assure herself that health was still predominant on her features. She assured herself of just that now as she touched her hair and straightened the set of exquisite pearls that graced her neckline. Her blue eyes dropped back to the soft woollen creation that was to be a matinee jacket for the newest family member-to-be, and she pondered whether it would be a boy or a girl - but only briefly: Sandra and Carl already had one of each, and as long as the grandchild was healthy, it mattered little what gender was increased. For safety, she had chosen a lemon colour.

The clock now read seven-zero-five, and she completed the next row and laid it down; went to the rather meagre kitchen and made a pot of tea. They would be here soon and she didn't mind admitting that she looked forward to their visit. The children had not been around for some time, but she understood – they had lives of their own to lead, and husbands to tend. Her own marriage had been a perfect one for half a century, and if her own children could be blessed with even half of that she would be very happy. It was their joys now that she could share in, her own having come to a rapid stand-still with Albert's demise five long years ago.

She carried the tea back into the lounge and put it on the small oval table by her chair, her eyes drifting momentarily out through the window to the street, to a passing car, but it wasn't them; not Sandra and Carl; not Judy and Simon; not Barry who had taken the notion to remain single and travel the world without restriction of wife or child, and who had taken special consideration to return to his homeland in time for her birthday. Not that he had said that, mind, but she knew that he had. He was a good boy, and she pondered that the next project would be a new sweater for her oldest, in blue because it matched his eyes, and he had inherited her eyes. Sandra had Bert's eyes she smiled solemnly, had Bert's every mannerism of face and mind, and his temper, and she was thankful Carl was a placid man. Judy on the other hand resembled none of them. Dark and broody, yet bright of mind and 'arty', Judy didn't talk much, but she was a keen listener and a deep thinker, and would probably one day be somebody special; what, she didn't know, but she would be. It was a mother's intuition to sense those things.

Glancing back over her shoulder, the clock showed ten past the hour, and she wondered if one of them would come early: Barry maybe. He had no family to hold him up, and he would relish the thought of not having to cook for himself. But then, Barry always had places to go and things to do, rushing here, rushing there. No, she decided wistfully, Judy would be the first for Sandra would be tied down with the infants, and with Carl for the man seemed to do little for himself, the product of an overly doting mother; something she was thankful that she had never been with her own. No, she considered proudly, she had been wise enough to let them find their own way in life, guiding them only along the paths of righteous belief, telling them the difference between right and wrong and leaving them to decide the road they would take. They had all taken the high road, and that made her proud.

The garment gained another inch and the clock another five minutes.

Soon, she pacified her anxiousness. *Don't hurry the children. They will arrive soon.* Her gaze flicked up to the dining table. It was ready, neatly set with an array of delectable dishes for supper; the usual cold dishes of chicken and salads, ham and slabs of lamb; nibblies of pretzels and peanuts and chips; and the trifle for Barry which he loved so much because she would always overladen it with sherry and wine. It was all there, all ready, and she was satisfied with the presentation. But they would need to be on time or it would all go warm and not taste as nice. For a moment she deliberated returning it to the refrigerator then decided not to worry. The clock said seven-twenty and another ten minutes would chill it no further than it already was.

Another inch lengthened the tiny jacket, the constant click of the needles tapping away with the seconds on the clock. Presently, Enid put down the bundle that busied her hands, patted her grey-gold hair into a more organised position and stood; she smoothed the sheeny cotton floral that she reserved for such occasions and, although a quiet thought told her not to, she wandered to the window to survey the tree-lined street below her sloping lawn. The clock clicked over seven-thirty, and at any moment one of them would arrive. Maybe even the next set of headlights coming down the road would turn and climb the driveway and stop beside the house.

None did, and for a long while no cars even came down the roadway. The street was dark and lonely, and soon not even the trees were distinguishable in the gloom. She noted her mood was rapidly beginning to match that of the atmosphere outside her window and she turned away and let her eyes take a slow wander over the room, a room where she seemed to be spending more and more time of late. Briefly she wondered if the children had felt as comfortable in this house as she had when they had moved there a decade ago. It was just she and Albert then, the children having grown and taken homes of their own. She consoled herself with the notion that they had seemed to have accepted the house though it hadn't been immediate, and she remembered the horrified looks on their faces when they had announced that the family home was to be sold, being far too large and difficult for her and Bertie to maintain in their senior years.

But they had gotten over it, she reflected lightly. They were good children, and only wanted what was best for her and their father, and now that it was only her, for her. A car appeared at the far end of the street, its golden cat-eyes casting a wide beam of light in its path, directing the way closer and closer to her daisy-strewn street verge. She watched keenly, waiting for the yellow blinker to flash its turning beacon, but it didn't — the car swept on past to become two minuscule slits of red until they too faded in the blackness. She sighed and glanced back to the clock on the cabinet. It was ten minutes to the next hour and she frowned, the motion adding to the creases already marring her otherwise unblemished face.

A nag of worry tinkered in her head as she turned back to the table, to the limping lettuce and sogging pudding. Scowling, she waited a few minutes more, took a nibble of a small morsel of bird, a peck of the wine-sodden cake, and returned the whole array of decorative bowls back to the ice-box. By eight o'clock, the needles were scraping and clicking noisily away again but this time without love-incited fingers: there was a greater need to be fulfilled inside her now, a need to alleviate the growing concern and quiet hint of annoyance. The hint grew rapidly to a more apparent thought that the needles did little to remedy. Had they forgotten? she wondered icily. And when had it been discussed that they would gather on this particular night, at this particular place? Or had she by chance taken for granted they would turn up as they always did, for none had ever forgotten her birthday before, and this one was special for it was her seventieth. Not sixty-eighth. Not sixty-ninth. But seventieth! And of course they would come! Maybe she had just mixed up the time, and they would be here soon. Maybe it was to be at eight. Of course, it was to be at eight. The children were seldom late, and certainly never all of them.

And so she waited, the needles again poised but inactive, her ear tuned to the silence on Wiggam Street. It remained unbearably so.

By eight-fifteen, she rose and poked her head hopefully into the kitchen, minor thoughts flitting to the teapot yet overshadowed by more pressing ones that prayed the lounge-room timepiece was wrong. Remorsefully, she sighed. It wasn't. Her knitting discarded to her favourite chair, she stood hollowly, fingers rubbing lightly up and down against confused temples, teasing out the slight but rising tension nagging at her brow. Turning, she looked forlornly about. It was eight-thirty, and obvious that she would have no visitors tonight, no-one to share her birthday with. Not her children. And not dear Albert, though memories of many better, fuller days of celebration glinted in and out of her reminiscences and made her smile.

There had been so many beautifully shared birthdays, so many filled with laughter and caring, what did it really matter that they had forgotten this one. She was not a selfish woman, she told herself as her hand found the light switch and dimmed that room, her knitting left to ponder the darkness, as alone as she herself felt right at that moment. No, she was not selfish, but she recognised that little pang of disappointment that hovered between her love for her children and her need to still be considered very much a part of the family, the part that kept them all together. She sighed deeply. It was time for this tired old lady to put herself to bed.

Tomorrow, she would be seventy and a day.

ȣ

The Breaker's Walk

Have you ever pondered the reasons that be
Why the Breaker walks with his knees in the breeze,
Why a whole day shines through between each slender thigh
Well I'll tell you the reason why.
But first you must note that the man is not addled
to want to spend all his days in the saddle,
But that's not the cause for the curve of his pants,
nor the awkward bow-legged stance.

Well you've heard how the old saying goes, of course
That the wildest of colts makes the best horse
It's the Breaker's job to make that come true,
But that's not so easy to do.
For they fight and they buck and they won't give an inch
resenting the band of the hard drawn up cinch
and the Breaker must stay astride of each toss
until he has mastered the hoss.

But it sometimes occurs that a horse lands a buck
that catches the Breaker down on his luck,
And strive as he may and fight as he must
Eventually he will bite the dust.
But it's part of the trade to know how to fall,
tuck up the limbs in a tight curling ball,
to limit the breaks avoids full defeat,
so he lands on the flesh of his seat.

Now it comes with the turf of the career he pursues
never to mention the size of the bruise,
So he grins and he bears it, rubs it and then
strides back to the horse and mounts it again.
Yet he knows by the ache in his shoulder and hip
and the fresh streak of red on his blooded top lip,
that a good horse will come from this wild bucking colt,
he could tell by the hard hitting jolt.

And he knows when it's done he'll feel old for his age
And he'll mutter his curses to lessen his rage
And he'll cringe in his legs and he'll walk with disdain
And it's all on account of the pain.
Now if you've ever been launched from the back of a hoss,
to land on your seat from the height of the toss,
if you've ever felt numb from the hard jarring hit,
even you may swear just a bit.

And well you might ask, how I know what I know,
Well, I apprenticed the Breaker for a year or so,
I learnt full his trade and the mode of his talk,
And I mastered the bow-legged walk.

&

The Cattle Dog

He wandered into town from the north, looking dusty and weary from long miles of travel. A tall man, the swag on his back and the dog at his heel gave the distinct impression he was a drifter. His blue eyes peered from beneath the wide brim of his faded hat, the sun's intensity causing him to squint as he sought out the location he needed most.

Further down the street - one which was wide and quiet, its verges gravelled to the stoops of shop fronts – he saw the Hotel, and sighed. Stepping up to the walkway in front of the stores, the little cattle dog padding in his wake, he headed that way.

It was Friday, which meant a few more people graced the street than at any other time of the week. Those that noticed him moved over and let him pass, paying more interest in the dog than in the man himself. A couple of the older station owners tipped their hats as he made his way to the drinking house further down the street. The man in turn tipped his politely back and kept walking.

"Nice friendly town," he said to the dog as he stepped down to another roadway and crossed over. Directly across the intersection stood the Hotel and his lips dried further, the annoying occurrence happening whenever he came close to quenching his thirst – it happened in towns, and it happened on the plains when sighting a water hole in the distance.

"Come on, Joe. If I can smuggle you inside, I'll buy you a drink."

Inside the Hotel, the young barmaid took no offence at the

presence of the dog. Its friendliness towards her rewarded it with a bowl of cool water. The man ordered something better for himself, and stood against the bar. Eyeing the establishment, he wondered if they had a spare room he could rent for a couple of days, and if so, would they allow the dog. If not, what were his alternatives?

Panning the bar, his eyes reached the front door, his interest catching as a rather sturdy police officer blocked the light at its opening. The constable's eyes held his for long seconds before they too slowly wandered around the room. The officer quickly assessed the presence of several of the town's familiar faces. His gaze then settled on the dog.

Staring for long moments, his brows dipping closely, he wandered forward and took a place at the bar beside the drifter.

"G'day," he said with a nod, his eyes deftly recording the younger man's features for later reference.

"G'day," the drifter responded, deliberately giving the man a similarly blatant perusal. He'd been in towns before where the constabulary didn't like drifters.

"Nice dog," the officer noted.

"Thanks," the drifter answered, turning back to the bar. He wondered for the first time what the interest was in the dog; remembered how the men on the street had paid it particular attention. He noted too that some of those men now stood as a group over by the Hotel doorway.

"His name wouldn't be Blue, would it?" the officer asked.

"No. I call him Joe," the drifter said, gazing straight ahead. He raised his glass and took a long drink. 'Something's definitely wrong,' he realised. 'Something about Joe's stirring the folk of this town,' and he didn't like the implication of trouble the questioning brought.

"Where'd you get him?" came the next query.

"Found him out on the trail about two weeks ago."

The Police officer looked from the dog to the man, his lips tightening. "I'm afraid I'm going to have to ask you a few more questions," he said, pulling a notebook and pen from his top shirt pocket, "and this time, it'll be for the record."

The drifter turned to him and looked puzzled. "Whatever you want," he said. "I've done nothing wrong."

"Name?"

"Bob Walters."

"Occupation?"

"Haven't decided yet."

The officer looked at him skeptically and scratched something down in the notebook. "You said the dog's name is Joe."

"I said, *I* call him Joe. I found him out towards Bria-bria, running with a dingo pack."

"You didn't see nobody out there running with him?"

"Nope. Just the dog, and the dingoes. Listen," the young man tired of the questions, "what's this all about?"

"Well son, this dog, if it happens to be the same one, belongs to one Jack Cooper, who we haven't seen nor heard of for over four weeks. Some folk here are mighty keen to know how you got hold of his dog when it would never leave his side."

Walters looked down at the dog. It was looking affectionately up at him, its blue-grey coat mottled with a tinge of red, whether from red heeler parentage or trail dust Bob didn't know. He'd just found the dog rather companionable, and suspected the dog felt the same about him seeing it had run to him at first sight, no hesitation in leaving the wild dogs whatsoever. It hadn't surprised him. With Joe's ribs showing prominently and his skin dry from dehydration, Bob knew he wouldn't have lasted much longer out there in the bush.

"All I know is, the dog came to me; and I've seen no-one out on the trail for several weeks. Maybe the dog jumped out of this Jack Cooper's car or something. Maybe Jack Cooper got sick of him and just dumped him. Why else would the dog be running around loose out there?"

"That's what we'd like to find out. You see, Jack was on his way out to do some stock work at Richardson's camp a month ago, but never arrived, and he's made no contact with anyone since he left."

"As I said," Walters reiterated, "I haven't seen anyone out there. Just Joe here."

Again the dog looked kindly up at the mention of his name.

"Did you see a horse roaming loose?"

The question came from one of the men further over, a tall, lean gent in his mid fifties.

"Nope. Only thing I saw similar was camels."

The police officer frowned. "You sure this is Jack's dog?" he asked the group of men. "It might just look like him."

"Call it Blue and you'll find out."

Stepping back to put more distance between him and the dog, the constable gave the men a 'here goes' look. "Blue!" he said.

Immediately, the cattle dog's head spun to the voice. Turning, it jumped up against the policeman, its tail wagging. The constable pushed it back to the floor, but the dog jumped up again and the constable had to be firmer in pushing it back to the floor.

"Joe!" another voice drew its attention away. The drifter's voice. The little cattle dog turned back instantly, sat down obediently by the man, its eyes looking keenly up. "You little traitor," the man said quietly, gruffly, though his hand went down to fondle its ears.

"Seems like it's Jack's dog all right," the country copper said, turning back to Walters. "Okay, exactly where did you find the dog?

We'd better send someone out to look for Jack."

Bob Walters described the ranges where the dingoes had been hunting, about two hundred miles up from Sampson's Plain. Another man confirmed that was a possible route Jack might have taken.

"Okay, we'll organise a search party," the police officer said. Then he turned to Bob Walters again. "I want you to stay in town until otherwise notified," he said. It was a subtle order, but an order just the same, and seeing he had nowhere else to go in a hurry, the drifter agreed. "I'll leave the dog with you, if you don't mind," he added more cordially before walking out.

"Nah. I guess I don't mind," Walters replied, his hand still resting on the dog's head.

Four days passed before the report came that Jack Cooper had been found, the news arriving at the same time as the group of local men gathered on the verandah of the Gundigindi Pub. As the local Sergeant described the find, the men looked dismayed.

"Old Jack's final hours slipped away beneath a lone tree out on the plains," the constable said. "The ashes of his campfire and the saddle at his side leads us to believe he died during the night, probably in his sleep. His horse had wandered off, but we found it by a water-hole, still hobbled. But still, it's luckier than Jack. At least it's still alive."

Discussion for a proper, decent burial started immediately, there being no family Jack ever spoke of to take care of the arrangements. Jack had worked for many of the men in the gathering, and all offered to help, the man's preference for being alone not hindering their friendship in any way. A 'Bushie' from way back, Jack was one of the 'old school', his family life and comforts forfeited for the solitude and bliss he found living on the trail.

"Ill take his horse and turn it out on the station where it can live out its days," one man offered promptly.

"And I'll make a stand so his saddle can be erected as a memorial in the Hotel foyer," the publican said. "We'll put a plaque on it in commemoration of the dying breed of Australians Jack was."

Leaning on a rail further down, Bob Walters listened to the plans, felt pleased for the old man. "He certainly was well liked," he remarked to Joe. "You must really miss him."

The dog looked up, its tail wagging at the man's tone. That was when one of the men looked over their way.

"What about the dog?" one station owner asked. "Who's going to take the dog?"

"I can't have it at my place," one reneged. "I've got a hoard of the damn things already."

"Nor can I," said another.

"Well," said the tall man in his fifties, looking around the group with a scowl, "I guess I'll have to have it, seeing I bred it."

The conversation made Walters go cold, then angry. The poor dog, destined now to live its life as an outcast, wanted in its puppyhood by a man who'd obviously loved it, but rejected in society simply because that man was no longer here. He'd heard enough.

Giving Joe a friendly shake of his neck fur, and a warm pat on its head, he bid the dog goodbye. He had stayed too long in one town already, and now realised why he had shunned humanity for the bush. People just didn't care. Not the way he cared. Not the way old Jack Cooper must have cared.

"Goodbye Joe," he said. "I wish you well however it turns out." He turned and walked away, leaving the dog on the verandah.

Walking a few steps, he stopped and turned back to check. Joe was following, as he'd followed him for weeks, padding the trails the old stockman had probably ridden many times before his death.

"No, stay!" he ordered, telling himself a drifter's life was no life for a dog; reminding himself of the difficulties a dog's presence would cause him, and wondering how Jack had faired with the problem.

The dog returned to the verandah as bid, its tail wagging slightly less as it waited for Walters to call it forward again. But he didn't. As Richardson on the verandah said, "Maybe it's best just to put it down. It'll probably go wandering off looking for Jack any way — these drover's dogs are just like their owners," he started walking, a deep breath inhaled at the words. This time he refused to look back. Poor Joe had no future. No future at all. He fixed his eyes on the south and walked with purpose, trying to put great distance between himself and the town and rid himself of the lump that had formed in his throat. The outback was no place for a dog.

At the far edge of town, a lone figure shouldered his swag and broke into the rambling gait that covered mile after endless mile. Still refusing to look back, unwilling to acknowledge the decisions being made in the town, he heaved a long sigh and pushed on, hoping his words weren't in vain.

"Nice to have you back, Joe," he said with dull acceptance, visualising the heeler's tail wagging as it faithfully dogged his steps.

&

The Eagle

I saw the eagle
deep brown majesty
soar aloft,
above the plains,
above yonder towering tree tops,
his wings borne wide,
and white tipped.
Wind ship.

Grandiose Lord of the skies
he flies
effortlessly,
master of that endless space,
a spirit to indigenous race
who hold him as a sign
of courage and strength,

Yet we of cult;
of no tribal lore;
stand only in awe
of his grace
of his kingdom and place
not realising that he holds the cosmic key
to being truly free.

Perfection,
in reflection,
he is
master of the wing,
of the wind,
of the land;
he has the admiration of man.

As I watch him
his wings in gentle windswept song,
strokes sky,
shadows land,
so grand;
so proud ...

I can see the eagle clearer now
Feel the eagle.
At one with himself.
Maybe too, if I try
I could be that eagle.

The Horse from Ethel Creek

There's a place in the north of Australia
where horses are bred for gain,
but they breed them in the wild
and leave for the Blacks to tame.
Now this place that's north and inland
is flat and green and vast;
it's known by most as Ethel Plain,
and there's a creek that flows right past.

Now the station owners are cluey there
and they know how to make a buck,
so they muster each year through to Brumby Creek,
send the catch down south by truck.
And the Big Smoke riders by them
for they know good flesh on sight
and they train them to play Polo
for they're swift and taut with might.

Now every so often, one is born
on the banks of Ethel Creek,
but they seem to be a different type
and it makes their future bleak,
for they have a reputation
of being solid, strong, but plain,
and even though they look quite grand,
they're lacking half a brain.

Now I heard of one that had been born
right on the river's tide
and it's been professed that this big colt
even the Blacks won't ride.
They shout out loud, "Not dis pella boss,
Dat bugga, him too hard."
Now I have the strangest feeling that
that bugger's in my yard.

He bucks, he rears, he bites, he kicks,
not a vice is left untested;
he gives it all with daunting strength,
much anger he has vested.
He's tough and strong, and lightning fast,
and not the slightest lazy.
It"s either that or I fear the worst,
and this blighter's downright crazy.

He'd been trucked down from pastures wild,
for Polo he was destined,
but it wasn't to be; the rider wised,
and his temperament was questioned.
So they left him on, drove further south,
a pub crawl they were taking;
till late that night a drunk did buy
this *polo-crosse horse in the making*.

Now this little horse had a mind of his own
and he'd loved the open plain,
and I'm sure he'd vowed not to ever submit
to play man's silly game.
Well to shorten the story a mile or so,
this rider soon came to me
saying, "You've got a name curing many a rogue.
Can you do this job for me?"

So I took it on, this little horse,
not knowing from whence it came;
a little horse with a wild eye
and a temper to match that acclaim.
So Billy the Black, my offsider,
led him off and away up the race,
came back and said, "Me no like dis one boss,
Got a mean ole look on him face."

So I said, "Don't worry, Billy,
I'll do this one alone.
You've taught me much over many years,
now my knowledge is full-grown."
Well he shot me a hard look in query,
was a look that would stir the dead,
and as he shrugged and turned, I heard him say,
"And so is da boss-woman's head."

But I didn't listen to the taunt,
I rode him while Billy looked on,
and I'd never sat such a fierce ride
as I got from that son-of-a-gun.
He broke my finger, cracked a rib,
ricked my neck and blooded my lip,
but I wouldn't yield to that fiery cur,
gasped air and restructured my grip.

And I yelled to Billy to 'let him loose',
needing room to stretch his bound
-- 'twas an old trick of Billy's for wilder brutes
-- run them into the ground.
And when they were tired you pushed them more
to be sure of their strength being spent,
then a quiet ride home to reward them;
no more nonsense or fighting dispensed.

So out through the gate we did gallop,
and into the pine forests long,
and we vanished from view in an instant,
his feet dancing out a quick song.
And onward and onward he bolted,
five mile flat strap we did race,
and I readied my spur for the moment,
and used them when he slacked the pace.

Another five mile we did travel
till he shook and was heaving for air
then I gently drew rein on the bridle,
to misfit more he'd not dare.
So I turned his head back to look homeward;
the lesson full learnt to this guy,
then off he did dash in an instant
and I knew I was going to die.

Ten mile we did bolt without lagging
his speed even greater to home
and he didn't flinch once to my pulling hands
while his mouth and body flecked foam.
And into my vision did enter
the homestead and yards did appear,
while I clung to my saddle, my lifeline,
my eyes and mouth wide with great fear.

And he soared o'er the sliprails so spritely,
while my hands made his mouth red and torn,
and I sailed o'er the gate to the garden,
landed flat on my back on the lawn.
Now Billy the Black wandered over,
a grin spread from ear to ear,
and he took up the reins of the mongrel
and over the gate paused to jeer.

"You did good, missie-boss, I can tell ya.
Him sure gotta fast way to run,
but I still say old Billy not ride him
'coz this old black pella not dumb."
Now my head is reduced in Billy's eyes;
my pride in myself is more humble.
But it took a big toss from that wild hoss
for my self esteem to crumble.

Well I crawled on my knees from the lawn to the house
and on hands pained and torn to the bone,
made the office desk, my whole body numb,
swallowed deeply and picked up the phone;
for there's a brand on that big colt's left shoulder,
who its owner I sought information,
and I wasn't surprised when they told me
it belonged to an Ethel Creek station.

Now I wangled a deal with colt's rider
and bought the horse just the same
but took Billy's advice and promised an oath
that this horse I would never tame.
And on days when it's cold and I ache in my bones
and my fingers and neck start to creak,
I look out to the yards and remember the day
I was trounced by the horse,
           The Horse from Ethel Creek.

❧

The Power of the Sea

Surging, swirling
bubbling wash of cyanic green boast
Churning, ebbing
Sweeping in to crash upon the rocky coast
Funnelling, gushing
an angry insurgent
Booming
through the chasm in resounding voice
Splattering
its very existence
in a spume of shattered atoms.
No choice.
Then courses back to renew its wrath
alive, and beating,
breathing ocean,
sending heartbeats pounding with emotion.

You are a trap
Yet what draws our minds?
Mesmerised,
I fall into your spell
and fall into the Albany Gap;
into the crushing tide.

Just another countless suicide.

The Prince of Wails

Cathy Gardner walked briskly down the wide polished corridor, her step in time with the brusque and rather British nurse who was to show her around, Matron being detained elsewhere in the Auxiliary Hospital.

"We call this wing Buckingham Palace," the woman told her tightly, "and we have a right royal time of here too I can tell you! In that ward there," she pointed to a door on the left in passing, "is no other than the Queen herself. Mrs, Eliza Tuttlebee, and Lord is she a prize! ... Expects us to bend and scrape to her every whim she does, and gives no thanks for our efforts. And you watch out for her daughter too," she warned in confidence. "The friggin' Princess expects a bloody cup of tea every time she comes to visit. I got her last time though, I did. 'This ain't no bleedin' coffee shop,' I told her, straight to her face I did. Well, you should have seen the look she gave me back. But not to worry, Love. Just don't let her push you around. They seem to hone in on you young ones."

They neared another door on the right, a private room by the name tag on the door.

"And here is the bloody Queen Mother. Right old tart she is. Catch cry of the day from that one is, 'Can I have some fresh flowers in here today. They do so brighten my day'," the woman mimicked disdainfully. "Well! As if she thinks I don't have enough to do without running out into the garden nickin' bloomin' flowers."

They crossed a junction of corridors, and continued on in the same direction.

"That's the Duke's room," she said, her fingers tapping lightly on the door as she passed. "He's not a bad old stick, that one... Doesn't speak to anyone – not a word has he peeped since he's been here ... the Love."

"How long is that?" Cathy asked, her thoughts having wandered to the old people in the Hospital.

"About two years," the nurse assessed quickly, seemingly undisturbed at the length of confinement. But that was probably usual, Cathy reflected – after all, it was an old people's Hospital. They grew too old to look after themselves then got shipped off here to die. She sighed at the sheer futility of it, swore that her mother and father would never see the inside of one of these places.

"Now for the finale ... The Prince of Bloody Wails," the Brit hissed out the words. "Mr. Bleedin' Johnson. He don't half gripe about everything. The tea's too hot. The food's too cold. The bed's too hard. Nothing makes him happy, nothing. No wonder his bleedin' kids don't come to see him. If he were my Dad, I certainly wouldn't come neither."

Cathy hoped she didn't have a Dad; thought that was a mean notion yet couldn't help it. Her attention was snapped back by a flashing light above Mr. Johnson's door.

"Oh dear, look at the time!" the portly nurse cried. "I'm going to be late for my tea break!"

With that, she hurried off back down the corridor along which they had come, pausing for the merest second to turn back. "The Recreation Room is at the end of the hall there. You just go on and see if anybody needs anything," she called.

"What about Mr. Johnson?"

"He can wait," she said, already on the move again.

Looking up, Cathy noted the light was still pulsing, waited until the nurse disappeared down another passage then knocked and entered.

"Yes, Mr. Johnson. May I help you?"

An old man well into his eighties sat hunched in a chair in the room's corner. He was withered with age, his thin face drawn with sagging jowls, the grey eyes somewhat clouded and definitely seeing not as well as they used to. The coffee table beside him held a cup and saucer within his reach.

"This tea's bloody awful," he whined, his harsh gaze on the rather pale-looking liquid. "And it's cold." He looked up, his eyes narrowing when failing to recognise her. "You're new here. I haven't seen you before," he grumped.

"No, Mr. Johnson, I only started today," Cathy told him. "Now let's see if I can't get you another cup of tea, one more to your liking."

"Won't do no bloody good," he griped, pouting as best he could.

"And why's that?" Cathy flashed him a keen eye.

"It always tastes bloody lousy. They don't have the brand Elsa and I used to buy."

"And what brand's that?"

"Wishmores ... the best bloody bush tea a man can get. Won't get it here though!"

"Why don't you get your children to bring some in when they visit," Cathy suggested, picking up his cup. "I'm sure the Staff will make it specially for you."

"Don't have no children," the old man huffed. "Els was never able to have kids. Bet she misses her Wishmores tea though."

"Where is your wife, Mr. Johnson?" the young woman asked, mystified that the old man was living alone.

"She took ill a while back," he jawed glumly. "They got her over in the next block, only take me to see her once a week. I'm afraid she looks so poorly." A tear touched his eye and he looked up. "She's so frightened you know. We've never been apart before, never in sixty years. Never had to suffer like this in our whole lives before." Then his anger rose.

"Damn small rooms; bloody frozen meals; beds like rocks! Nobody cares ... Nobody cares."

Cathy felt remorsed by his sad situation. "Why won't they let you see your wife more often, Mr. Johnson?"

"Because they're too bloody lazy. Oh, they say they've no time, too few nurses as it is," he related venomously. "It's not fair! Not fair that I'm imprisoned here!" He thumped his fist on the arm of the chair.

Cathy propped herself down on the edge of the bed, knew instantly why he thought it was hard, and looked at him warmly. "I think I can help you, Mr. Johnson," she told him. "You see, I'm a Hospice Volunteer, and I spend my time visiting people such as you, making sure everything is okay. Now, if you like, and if I can clear it with Matron, I can organise that you can see your wife every second day. Would you like that?"

"Would I?!" the old man gushed.

"Good, then I'd better get to it. First, your cup of tea, hot to start with rather than Wishmores, then I'll go and see Matron, and pop out into the garden before I go and see Mrs. ... ah ... Mrs. ..."

"The Queen Mother," Mr. Johnson smiled, catching the Volunteer by surprise. "I'm the Prince of Wails, you know."

✒

The Magic of Christmas

There's a trail of silver across the sky
it's reindeer dust left when they fly
drawing Santa's sleigh around the world
on his Christmas run to every boy and girl.

This trail of silver left from feet
which dance across the night, discreet
in how they touch the earthy ground
careful lest they careless bound
on roofs and fall inside;
where there's not a place to hide.

And if you're good in silent phase
you might hear the prancing ways
of golden hooves upon your roof
and Santa with his jovial laugh
as down he slides to leave a gift
hung on your mantelpiece aloft.

And watching closely through the door
why, there's silver dust upon the floor
and looking out through window bright
there's silver dust across the night
as reindeer prance back to the sky
Give them a wave and say a soft Goodbye

And smiling know the silver trail
is not as told, a snail's trail
It's where Old Nick and reindeer pals
have visited the boys and gals
and know this silver's magic treat;
it's flying dust for reindeer feet.

The Remember Game

Daisy picked her way through the hummock and spinifex as she headed down to the stream, a small pale hand encased in hers. "We gunna play remember game," she said to the child trudging along beside her. "We gunna turn dis ting round."

They reached the stream that rippled slowly towards the distant gorge, its pebbly base glinting like diamonds where the water coursing round the curve had deepened the stream to calf deep. Here Daisy had built a containment pond, where she soaked Zamia seeds for February eating. The water gathered in the pool, swirled around before swelling up and trickling over rocks to continue on its way. She scooped the still rock-hard Zamia seeds out of the small round pool and laid them on the bank, freeing the pool for the game.

"Okay, you take off dem old boots and put 'em up on dis big pella rock. I don't want your Dad gettin' narky at me ip you gettem wet."

The child sat in the red dust and peeled off her scuffed, brown boots and orange tinged socks, and sat them on the rock as Daisy said.

"Okay, now you go in da water dere, and take dat basket wib ya." She scooped some of the basket's contents out into her orange-stained, floral skirt, gathered up the hem to her waist and climbed onto the boulder beside the stream. The child waded into the stream which swirled gently around her knees, eradicating the smudges of red dirt that had gathered on her pink skin during their walk from the homestead.

Daisy turned and sat, her calloused bare feet sticking out on the warm ochre surface further heating in the sun. "You ready," she grinned. "Me pirst." She thought for a moment then said ... "I remember ..." Her head tipped slightly as the past filtered to her mind. "Yeah, I know ... I remember dat day you tried to cut across da home paddock to get to the muster camp across da riber and dat bloody old big pella bull Bossman put in there chased you right up dat skinny gimlet tree. I still remember da way your skinny legs looked turning circles like Curly's old bike ya ran so fast and how ya had to lift 'em high to leap above the tall brown grass. Geez, I had to hang on to da fence to stay standin' up ya looked so bloody funny."

Her big white grin gleaming from her ebony face and the way her plump high cheeks lifted invoked the child's wide smile. She stood looking up at Daisy, all sweetness and dusty brown curls. "Dem legs just went round and round and round," Daisy added, grinning wider, her arms churning like huge locomotive wheels as she emulated how the wildly flailing legs moved. Her actions made Missy giggle.

Then Daisy remembered and plucked a flower from the folds of her skirt, held its stem in her fingers, twirled it then let it fly spinning through the air until it drifted down and settled on the water. It lingered a moment then was picked up by the swirling flow and danced around the pool. "Now, it's your turn," she said, glad of the child's glee.

Missy watched the flower bobbing around on the pool. "I remember ... I remember," she sifted carefully, so many memories flooding in, "I remember when you taught me to tie my bows." Her eyes lit with the joy of that moment so long ago. "... and you got my finger stuck in the laces, and you said ... 'Well, how did that happen?' And so you showed me again ... and you got my finger stuck again! And you pulled a funny face and I laughed and laughed and laughed."

Daisy started to chuckle too. "Flower! Flower!"

Missy picked a flower from the basket and carefully laid it on the water, watched as it swirled around and caught the same circular motion as Daisy's.

"My turn," Daisy grinned, images already dancing in her mind. "I remember da first day I taught ya how to make bread. You got more of dat belly flour across da table and up da kitchen walls than ya got in the bread dough. Then Bossman came in and roared with laughter 'cose you had dough on ya face and flour in ya hair and he grabbed ya round the waist and whirled ya round and said dat ya looked good enough ta eat. You remember dat?"

Missy squealed: "I remember that," gladness painting colour back onto her face.

"Oh I laughed and laughed," Daisy remembered.

She picked another flower from her skirt basket, held it up, twirled it and let the wind take it to the pond. Missy watched it soar, spinning on its descent, followed its arc down to join the others. Missy laughed too. Then she said: "I remember when you tried to teach me to ride and Mr Magic started running fast and I went bounce, bounce, bounce and bounced right off his back onto the ground. And you ran over and picked me up and said: 'Now, how did that happen?' And you made me laugh when I really wanted to cry because it hurt so much – and I'm sorry I wouldn't let you try to teach me again. Then Daddy said he would teach me to ride and you could teach me later when you learnt to ride first. I really, really liked it when we finally got to go out riding together."

Daisy sighed deeply. "Yeah, dat was real nice."

Missy picked another white flower from the basket and laid it gently on the water. It drifted and bobbed and surged around the pool to join the others.

Daisy was deep in thought when Missy called out: "Remember another one, Daisy. Remember another one."

Daisy nodded, enjoying the images that poured into her head.

She grinned widely, pulled out the next flower and gazed at it. "I remember da first day you come to Kyeema in dat beat up old Landbrover. It done pull up in a big bloody cloud ob dust and you climbed out coughin' and wheezin' and cubered in dirt. We all be standin' on da verandah and you looked up at dat big old homestead and said: 'Oh my God!' We done taut you'd get straight back in dat bloody rattly car and go back where you come from. I always remember da look on your face dat day." She smiled but a tear rose to the corner of her eye and she sighed then sat staring out across the mulga plain on the other side of the creek.

"Your frangapelli, Daisy ... Throw your frangapelli."

"Frang-i-pani," Daisy corrected, remembering how Bossman had taught her the names of the flowers in the homestead garden, this giant tree constantly spattering the ground and its canopy with white and yellow blooms. She loved lying under the thick shady branches staring up at the sun when Boss Lady had nothing for her to do. Sometime she'd sit out there with her too.

"Daisy ..."

Daisy snapped back to the moment, selected the largest flower and twirled it onto the wind. Missy watched as its wide curved petals turned elegantly as it made its way down to the water. The flowers had now all gathered near the bank where Daisy had laid the Zamia seeds, each turning on the gentle motion of the water like ballerinas pirouetting on pointy toes.

"Your turn."

Missy sighed deeply; sighed again. "I remember when you got sick ..."

"No! Not dat one," Daisy ordered brusquely. "Something else ... you hab to remember something nice."

Missy thought for a short time. "I remember, " she said wistfully, "when you used to tuck me into bed and read me a story, and when you were finished you'd kiss me goodnight right here." She pointed to the middle of her forehead, "... and I'd put my arms around your neck and give you the big, big, biggest hug."

Daisy smiled; smiled ever so slightly. "Dat one 'serbs two flowers," she said.

Missy carefully picked two beautiful yellow-centred blooms and laid them on the water. Their dance joined the corps de ballet and around the pool they twirled. "Aren't they beautiful," Missy said, watching them bob and whirl and partner off in a gentle, graceful waltz. Finally she said, "Your turn, Daisy!"

"Okay, last one but," she said, "or Bossman gunna wonder where we got to." She edged herself from the rock to stand in the cool wet sand. "I remember dat day when Bossman sold all dose big pella bulls. He was so bloody proud he picked you up and spun ya round on da big verandah and you and Bossman started dancin'. Geez you dance funny, all slow and twirly and squashed in togedda." She spun around with one arm in the air. "I'd neber seen dancin' like dat before."

"Daddy calls it waltzing, like waltzing Matilda."

"Yeah, like we better be waltzin' back to da house," said Daisy, wading in to the stream. She stood with Missie watching the white flowers dance around them. "You ready set dem mem'ries free? Let dem fly to the bush so all da spirits can hear all da happy stories?"

Missie nodded, her curls bouncing across her shoulders.

"Okay, you say a wish now and we let 'em go so dem stories can be told all across the land. You got a wish?"

Again Missie nodded with excitement.

"Okay, say your wish." Daisy lifted a rock and let the stream pour out through the opening. The current picked up the flowers and carried them round in a circle and out through the gap, took those dancing frangipanis floating away down the river, a row of ballerinas twirling on their points.

"I wish you will always be happy," Missie said, watching the flowers glide away, each one a beautiful memory she would always remember. She looked up at Daisy, waiting for her wish.

"And I wish you always be happy," Daisy said, looking down at the little girl.

They watched a moment longer then Daisy dropped the Zamia seeds back into the soaking pool, helped Missie pull on her boots and together they wandered back through the scrub to the homestead, the little girl skipping at times to keep up with Daisy's long stride. "Do you think we can bring Daddy to play the Remember Game next time?" she asked Daisy cheerily. "I think Daddy would like to remember Mummy too then maybe he won't be sad anymore."

Daisy squeezed Missie's tiny hand. "Dat's a real good idea," she said solemnly, looking down at the child and appreciating the life coming back in those big blue eyes. "Dat's a real bloody good idea."

&

The Trouvere and the Troubadour

He walked the lands with words galore
spouting them with nuance pure
reciting epic fabliaux;
That valiant trouvere.

Composing verse he strut the land,
pen and palette in his hand;
he glorified the deeds of man,
That valiant trouvere

Until in Trouvelle Port he came
upon the Troubadour acclaimed,
of estaminet he was long fained,
That sotted Troubadour.

The Troubadour with lyre strung
attuned words of the trouvere's tongue,
these words he said he'd wrote and sung,
That sotted Troubadour.

Yet trouvere did not raise his ire,
he kowtowed low and took the lyre
and strumming strings he did aspire
to mock that Troubadour.

'Twas in the vale of Arbonne,
at close of inn on Festive day
that you, kind sir, did hear me ply
my wordsmith trade near thee.

You stole my verse, you faitor born,
I break your lyre, strung but worn,
I now redeem my work with scorn,
said valiant Trouvere.

Now scour away your sozzled name
from on my words which brought you fame;
I revoke your long attested claim
to the words of bold Trouvere.

And so the proud Trouvere did go
wandering long, reciting slow;
no more did singer steal his show,
That valiant Trouvere.

&

Wild Roses

Wild vining roses twined up the white ornamental lattice-work of the old cottage in deepest Innesvale. In brilliant shades of pale red and gold, they grew in glorious profusion. Densely bracked and glossy leaved, they faced the spring sunshine, their petals dew-kissed by the early morning mists that lingered long in the valley. Their tendrils twisted outward from the woodwork, curved downward, hovering to catch each life-giving droplet of dew and ready to attach to whatever came within their determined reach. Cascading from the eaves in heavy clusters, and from the sides of every verandah post, they were most prolific at the newels at each side of the steps.

"Angry little buggers," Mal Ryborg hissed as he unhooked his arm from the claws of a particularly straggling runner. A speck of blood trickled from the minute nick it left upon his arm.

He stepped up to the verandah and finger-lifted another bract aside so Merilee could pass by its reach unmarred.

The verandah was cool, wide and shady, a pleasance he promptly noted. It would easily accommodate their white, six-seater setting, and allow them to enjoy quiet evenings sitting out in the scenery. At least until they sold the place.

He glanced around and saw his wife taking in all that surrounded them; steeled as she drew a deep and languid sigh.

"Oh Mac, we could spend an eternity gazing at crimson sunsets out here," she swooned, her eyes settling on the myriad of blooms that clung to that atrocious vine. (She had always called him 'Mac'. It was easier than the confusion caused by her brother's name also being Malcolm, and he being called Mal.)

"They'll have to come down first," he proffered, fingering the trail of blood now trickling down his arm. He noted how intensely the minute wound still stung.

Merilee looked instantly at the emerald leaves and saw them quivering. "Oh no, Mac!, you mustn't touch the roses. They're so beautiful. And they give the house such wonderful character, such old world charm."

"They block the light to the house and make it cold," he retorted as he turned towards the large front door. Jesus! He knew she could be earthy, but this was beyond a joke.

Behind him, a long twisted tendril reached out for his throat, but Merilee caught it gently and eased it back. "No, not yet," she whispered. Her hand gently caressed the well-thorned limb. "Not yet."

"... and besides, their thorns are so damn sharp; I don't want to be a mass of lacerations each time I come within coo-ee of the place." His arm indeed was stinging greater, a deep burning sensation spreading down into his hand. "Shit this hurts ... Furthermore, you might as well get used to it, Mer, because this place will need a real good clean up before we sell it."

A sudden gust of wind blew up and coursed along the verandah as Merilee's eyes flew wider. Her jaw dropped slack.

"Sell it! We can't sell it! This was Grandma's house!"

The wind reached the rose vine and sent a bract of it lashing across Mac's cheek. It tore a fine line from his nose and drew back to his ear. "Ah! What the ..."

His hand went to the warm flow of liquid searing his torn flesh. "Jesus Christ, did you see that? Shit! Damn it!" He removed his hand and inspected the amount of blood staining his palm red. "Now do you see why I want to get rid of these things. They're bloody lethal."

His wife looked astounded at how quickly the events had turned, as her husband plopped into one of the old wicker chairs that already graced the verandah. He lent forward, trying to contain the pain with one hand as he reached for the handkerchief in his pocket with his other.

"Mac ..." Merilee's hands fell to her side. "Mac, the roses *have* to stay."

He looked up at her, his eyes revealing no signs of relenting. "So, it matters little to you that they just ripped my face off and have probably scarred me for life? Mer ..."

"They were my grandfather's roses! And this was Grandmother's house. These roses are all that is left of him. That's why I cannot let you destroy them."

"So they *do* mean more to you than I!" He mopped another seepage of blood and endeavoured to pinch the gaping edges of his reddening cheek together. "You amaze me sometimes, Merilee ... You really ama..."

"You don't understand," she wailed. "These roses were planted when Grandmother and Grandfather were married. Do you know how old that makes them?"

"About old enough to let them die a graceful death!"

The rose bush shook violently. Its gnarled limbs almost visibly moved on the trellis. Mac rose and walked to the steps of the verandah, warily ducking beneath the swaying bract of thorns that arced his way as he stepped down to a lower level.

"This place would look much neater without all these cluttering the front. You're just going to have to be reasonable for once, Merilee. And there's no way I intend to ever live here. Not permanently anyway. It's much too far from work."

He took the last step down to the lawn as another spiked swipe narrowly missed his neck. "If we have to stay here it will only be until we find a buyer, because I certainly don't want to spend the rest of my life living in a pre-century cottage going backwards the rest of our lives!”

He didn't look back as he walked away down the path, Merilee's hand catching the vine as it struggled hard to reach him.

“No, my pet; Grandpa's little Precious. You must be patient,” she soothed. The vine wafted airily for a moment then landed lightly on her shoulder, gently fluttered there until she carefully detached it and placed it back on the rail. “Grandpa's little Precious must be very careful this time. And never ... never be sighted from the street.”

The woman who stepped down from the verandah looked somewhat older than the mild, young woman who had climbed it minutes before. Her eyes were darker now, sunken, her skin heavily lined and dry. Her pouting lips were creased with sudden age.

“I will not sell this house!” she bellowed after Mac as he disappeared round the corner, heading towards the backyard. Her voice was harsh like a rasp. “I will never sell!”

“You'll see reason soon enough,” his voice drifted back to her. “Once the roses are gone, you'll see reason.”

A loud scream emitted from that side of the house, muffled grossly for a moment then was cut short. The rose trellis started rustling loudly, their leaves trembling fiercely in the swift rising wind. The pale red roses slowly developed a more vivid hue, deeper bloodier red. Then all was still.

On the verandah the old crone, rebirthed by the touch of the vine, her kin rekindled, stood cackling at her newfound widowhood. It was again now just her and her husband's 'Precious' roses. He too had never suspected the secret of his toil, the hunger of the seeds, until it was far too late.

⃠

Achievements

All in the Family	First Place in the National Horror Writers Competition
Any Place	Commended in the Ethel Webb Bundell Literary Awards 2012
A Time For Dawn	Commended in the Katharine Susannah Prichard Open Awards 2010
Battle Beach – 6th of June	Commended in The Society of Women Writers WA Bronze Quill 2008
Behind the Scenes	Commended in The Society of Women Writers WA Bronze Quill
Brave Molly	Commended in The Society of Women Writers WA Bronze Quill
Crocs on the Highway	Published in Readers World magazine
Devachan	Published in Readers World magazine
From a Blanket	Published in Galloping On anthology
From the Steps of Bradley Street	Published in Readers World magazine
hoops	Commended in The Society of Women Writers WA Bronze Quill 2014

In Bradley's House	Winner of The Society of Women Writers WA Bronze Quill 2010
Island Time	Second Place in The Society of Women Writers WA Bronze Quill 2013
Just a Doll and a Story	Commended in The Society of Women Writers WA Bronze Quill 2007 Highly Commended in The Port Stephens Examiner Literature Awards 2011
Kimberley Dream	Special Mention in The Society of Women Writers WA Bronze Quill 2011
Listen	Published in the International Poets Society anthology Portraits of Life
Moments	Highly Commended in The Society of Women Writers WA Bronze Quill 2013
Much Ado About Nunning	Winner, Best Film Idea – The Scarlet Stilleto competition 2012
Neither Lie, Douglas	Published in Penfriends Magazine
On 66th Street	Commended in the Tom Howard Short Story competition
Resolutions	Highly Commended in The Society of Women Writers WA Bronze Quill 2004
Serpent River	Commended in The Society of Women Writers WA Ethel Webb Bundell Literary Awards 2016
Study Time	Published in Armadale High School magazine

The Birthday	Winner of The Society of Women Writers WA Bronze Quill 2007
The Breaker's Walk	Commended in the Henry Lawson competition
The Cattle Dog	Highly Commended Award Writer's World
The Eagle	Outstanding Award Writer's World competition
The Horse from Ethel Creek	Winner ABC Regional Radio Poetry competition
The Power of the Sea	Published in Readers World magazine
The Prince of Wails	Published in The Society of Women Writers WA Anthology
The Magic of Christmas	Published in National Library Christmas Book
The Remember Game	Second Place in The Society of Women Writers WA Bronze Quill 2013
The Trouvere and the Troubadour	Published in Galloping On anthology
Wild Roses	Published in Readers World magazine

&

About the Author

Western Australian born author Helen Iles writes in all genres. Her love of the State's Northwest and her strong background in training horses features through many of the stories and poems in this anthology.

A Creative Writing tutor, Helen writes adult and children's fiction, text books and poetry, and provides manuscript assessment and editing services. She conducts writing workshops between penning new stories, poems and novels and entering the occasional competition.

www.ingramcontent.com/pod-product-compliance
Lightning Source LLC
Chambersburg PA
CBHW071013180726
48291CB00004B/1436